W.

St Andrews
Ghost Stories

Fiction

1911

Plus

THE STRANGE STORY OF ST ANDREWS HAUNTED TOWER

Nonfiction

1925

By
Dean of Guild
W. T. LINSKILL

Introduced, annotated and illustrated by
RICHARD FALCONER

Published in association with
St Andrews Ghost Tours

Cover design and content layout by Richard Falconer

OBSIDIAN
BOOK PUBLISHING
www.obsidianpublishing.com
enquiries@obsidianpublishing.co.uk

Also available by Richard Falconer

Nonfiction / Paranormal / Educational
More Ghosts of St Andrews

The most complete published record of people's paranormal
experiences anywhere for one location.
133 new St Andrews locations, 260 ghosts, 314 experiences

Nonfiction / Paranormal / Educational
Ghosts of St Andrews

Incorporating 65 St Andrews locations

Nonfiction / Paranormal / Educational
A St Andrews Mystery

*An Investigation into the Chamber of Corpses and the White Lady
Apparitions of St Andrews*

Nonfiction / Paranormal / Educational
Ghosts of Fife

The only book devoted to the paranormal in Fife
Incorporating over 80 places throughout the Kingdom

Coming soon

Nonfiction / Global Paranormal / Psychology / Educational
Ghosts

The Mechanics of the Paranormal
The reality of global phenomena beyond empirical science

Nonfiction / Paranormal / Educational
Pocket Guide to St Andrews Ghosts

A small compendium of 198 haunted locations

Nonfiction / Local History / Educational
History of St Andrews

Focusing on the 6th to 17th Centuries AD

𝔇edicated to the memory of

the Dean of Guild W. T. Linskill
1855 to 1929

Author, Golfer, Poet, Actor, Orator, Caricaturist,
Antiquarian, Councillor, Dean, Magistrate & Father

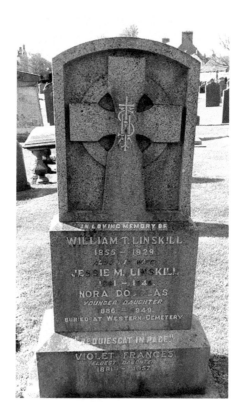

His grave is just north of the high altar in the
Cathedral grounds

Introduced by
Richard Falconer

The Dean of Guild

William Thomas Linskill

Born in 1855, he was the son of Captain William T. Linskill of Tynemouth Lodge, Northumberland, who was educated at Harrow and Captain of the 5th Dragoon Guards, and the Honourable Mrs Frances Arthur Charlotte Linskill, daughter of Arthur Annesley the 10th Viscount Valentia, a title in the Peerage of Ireland. The family had their origins as a powerful Anglo-Irish family between the County of Buckinghamshire and the County of Armagh.

Linskill studied at the Jesus College, Cambridge and was known at the time as both 'Tommy' Linskill and 'Mr Cambridge'. It was Linskill who formalised the game of golf in Cambridge. After becoming a member of the Royal and Ancient Club House in 1875, he founded the Cambridge University Golf Club (CUGC) in the same year from the ashes of an unofficial body formed some six years previous and no longer active. He was Captain of the Club and Honorary Secretary for 20 years. He also united Oxford and Cambridge in golfing tournaments forming the Oxford and Cambridge Golfing Society. The society is known to be the oldest golfing society in the world, with their first 'Varsity' match being played on the 6th March 1878. The photograph on the previous page was taken in Cambridge on one of these golfing outings. In the background are members wearing the blue blazers and crest of his Cambridge Golf Club.

Besides *St. Andrews Ghost Stories*, Linskill wrote one of the earliest books about the history of golf. Published in 1889, and simply titled *Golf*, it was written very much from a St Andrews perspective as an early beginner's guide based at the Links, and includes 19th century techniques and rules of play.[i]

Linskill often visited St Andrews with his parents when he was young and looked forward to playing a round of golf whilst here, but he never moved here until 1877. He continued to travel for matches in Cambridge through his life and to carry out his official duties with the club and society. He lived for a time in Deans Court opposite the Cathedral and spent many a night wandering its precincts in search of the illusive he so lovingly wrote about. He also lived in newly built 17 Murray Park with his wife and two daughters. The houses being built on former parkland.

Linskill was a town councillor for over twenty years, becoming the Dean of Guild and local magistrate. Contributing greatly to the furtherance and well-being of St

---

[i] The book includes some of the early commentaries to have been written about the game of Golf. The period featured is from 1801 to 1889. Centred on St Andrews it makes fascinating reading for any interested in the game and its early development in the town.

Andrews, he constantly battled for the town against eternal steadfast opposition by fellow councillors unwilling to change their early Victorian ways. A problem Tom Morris also faced with the R & A in trying to advance the game of golf. It was Linskill who introduced the first fire service to the town. The fire engine was a steam engine with rows of hooks for buckets. It caused quite a sensation as few had ever seen such an elaborate contraption before.

Linskill was a well-known and well-respected character both in Cambridge and St Andrews – well, as much as any Victorian Gentleman of standing can be, although his stern enthusiasm was known to ruffle the odd feather or two!

An article written when he was still alive said of Linskill: 'The artistic life of St Andrews holds no more interesting figure than that of the Dean. His services to the St Andrews of another day in the development of its dramatic talent will not soon be forgotten.'

He certainly was a character. In addition to being an author, he had a great memory and was a renowned raconteur. In many ways, there are similarities between Linskill and the celebrated golf historian David Joy in our present age. Both well known to the town, both known for spinning a yarn or two, and both sought after for their after-dinner speaking abilities. Linskill relished in telling his ghostly tales as after dinner stories in Cambridge, St Andrews and no doubt wherever he happened to find himself over the years. Both David and Linskill were actors, performing in local St Andrews plays, they both have a great passion for the game of golf from an early age, and both have written about the game.

David occasionally assumed the character of Old Tom Morris, while Linskill prided himself on his golfing partner and tutor being four-time Open Golf Champion - Young Tom Morris. An article recorded that if the two Tom's were in St Andrews and it was a full moon, they would set off and

play the Pilmour Links (the Old Course) at night when it was dark! They both had a humour and would employ the services of five caddies for their nocturnal pursuits for perfection. Four caddies to look for the balls and one behind pushing a wheelbarrow full of refreshments (bottles of port) for their task in hand. I can just imagine them playing a few holes, then on realising they were running out of port, turning about and playing in to the R & A.

Both Linskill and David also share a penchant for the odd spirit, while Linskill also enjoyed another form...

Linskill and his Spirits

Linskill had an unshakable passion for ghosts and the paranormal in general. He would dearly loved to have seen a ghost himself. Alas they were to prove as illusive to his experiences as the conviction of their reality to the sceptic. He attributed his lacking in direct experience to simply not being psychic. He never felt he was in possession of these attributes. In an article to the *Citizen* in 1917, he says, 'I very much regret that I live on some wrong "spiritual plane," and am absolutely unable to see these things, whatever they are, even in the most haunted castles and houses.'

He was like the majority in that respect. Spiritual abilities are part of everyone's psyche but few realise it, so when the unusual occurs they are easily misappropriated or shrugged off. Ghosts are all about being in the right place, right time and more often looking in the right direction. In a way they form the blunt end of our awareness spectrum when it comes to occult abilities. The subtleties of intuition, precognition, psychometry, mind over matter &c, will only be made apparent with an open mind, a quality of itself as rare as these abilities many look to decry. Linskill had an open mind, but he was also caught in this web of conditioned denial in not being able to recognise his own. In one of his stories, he also mentions having never heard a ghost – but he did. Linskill ended up at the top of St Rules Tower or Square Tower as it is known, at midnight on his own one Halloween. It was the result of a wager by one of his fellow roommates that one of them wouldn't spend a couple of hours alone at its top. Not that they were all looking at Linskill of course, but he was first to rise to the challenge. With his necessary supply of brandy and cigars to see him through his impending ordeal, he boldly ventured to the tower.

There are two ghosts along with various impressions of monks from an earlier time in the tower. One is a Greyfriars monk, the other, which few are aware of is the White Lady in the upper windows. Along with the Haunted Tower this is one of three locations, possibly four, where she has been seen. I saw here with a party of nine elderly people on a tour from Austria in 2015. They were on the tour for the history, and had no interest in ghosts at all. They all saw the figure and were just appeasing me when I prompted them to try and take photos. For ten minutes we snapped away but it was too dark, too far away, and to them it was just a woman looking out of the window. They didn't believe me when I said there was no floor behind the window. If they had gone into the tower the following day and looked up, their lives would have changed forever. The tower is hollow.

Linskill obtained the key to the tower from the Cathedral's Keeper of Keys. On locking the tower door behind him, he climbed the steep spiralling steps to the top. He would have looked more in place had he been wandering into a beer garden than up the tower with brandy and cigars in hand, but what more could any aspiring ghost hunter possibly require! Oh, he did also take sandwiches.

On reaching the top, he complied with the terms of the wager and remained there for exactly two hours. He sat at the top of the stair with his bravado for company, which soon began lacking the eagerness witnessed by his friends back in the comforts of their warm brightly lit lodgings.

From his report the experience terrified him! Despite there being no one else in the tower, he knew he was not alone. Whilst at the top he heard footsteps of someone walking up the tower, he called out a few times, but no one replied and no one ever arrived at the top. When his two hours were up, and with a sigh of relief, he began making his way down the spiral stone steps. As he did so, he again heard the same footsteps, but this time they were coming from above. Someone was now following him down. He stopped, but the footsteps continued and again no one arrived. When he returned to the ground, he locked the door and made his way back to the Keeper of the Keys, where he gladly received a very stiff whisky – having I imagine already demolished his supply of brandy by the time he made it to the top of the tower.

Linskill was unaware of the White Lady in St Rule's, but would dearly loved to have seen the monk, although, given how terrified he was that Halloween night, such an experience may have been the end of him!

While his conviction for their reality was unshaken despite not visually experiencing anything, he was sceptical to some aspects of Victorian spiritualism, as were many of the day following exposés of fraudulent practices being publicised in the national and international press. In public, the sceptics used this to denounce the practice and the subject, but he saw through this lame façade. He knew this was a mask by charlatans exploiting the vulnerable and overshadowing genuine mediumistic ability. A view shared at the time by Sir Arthur Conan Doyle and Harry Houdini. Houdini's strong conviction for its reality resulted in him spending most of his life exposing fraudulent mediums whilst on tour. He was certainly qualified to do so, Houdini began his career as a fraudulent medium before venturing into the world of escapology. What fraudsters did do, was to divide opinion for its reality to about 40/40 with about 20% not sure, which is where it remains to this day in both the UK and the States.

Gathering information

Linskill was a great collector of supernatural tales or yarns as he often described them. Despite his lacking in personal experience, he knew of their reality through those in his acquaintance. He enjoyed the company of the town immensely, usually from the comforts of the New Bar in the Star Hotel, where he became familiar with local ghost lore and some of the shades he would later feature in his stories. I never used to think recognising genuine experience to be a gift, but when the majority appear unable to do so, it is unmistakably the case. It is all the more compelling when backed by further independent testimony, especially by those visiting the town with no prior knowledge of the ghosts here.

Linskill's style and appeal

Being old school, Linskill doesn't appeal to those who forget his stories were written by a Victorian mind for a Victorian mind. This was an age when ghost stories were finding their ground and electricity was still a luxury. On saying this, technology makes us think we are advanced, but technology hasn't changed our basic instincts in over 5000 years. As a functioning species, we remain the same today as we did then. Fear of the dark has always been an instinctual trait and the Victorians had a lot more darkness in a literal sense than we do now. In a metaphysical sense, the opposite is also true, the more reliant we are on material concerns, the darker we become to our true potential beyond physical advancement.

Atmosphere

Setting the scene in his narrative was certainly part of Linskill's formula. He loved to promote a conducive and congenial atmosphere.

Linskill transports the reader through an echo in time, commanding all the airs and graces of Victorian fireside storyteller, liberally mixed with his inimitable jovial style. His manner is always pleasant to the senses in this respect and warming to the imagination. His humour is both entertaining and fanciful, and filled with all the indulgence, flamboyance and appeal of a Victorian gentleman.

Mythological status

Linskill may not match the literary prominence of Stoker, James, Le Fanu, Shelley or Poe &c of the time, but it was Linskill who gave St Andrews most of the ghost stories it has. They have left a profound mark on the psyche of the town. So much so, we have an extensive panoply of history and plenty of mystery, but without Linskill's stories there would be little mythological tradition in St Andrews outside the political marketing spin of church denominations decrying their opposition.

Fact or Fiction?

Linskill's stories appear to be a collection of Victorian supernatural fiction, and fictional stories in themselves, like myths and legends, rarely hold up to historical scrutiny. However, elements of truth often reside at their heart, and that is what we have here.

Over the years I have looked to see if there are any nuggets of fact in Linskill's stories. The way of doing this has been through correlating experiences with his writing to find where the fiction ends and the facts begin. This has been an unfolding process spanning six decades so far, and it never ceases to surprise. The conclusion I have come to is his stories comprise nine parts fiction and one-part fact. There is the occasional fact hidden amongst his background stories, but for the most part his stories are fiction, so the one-part fact comes in the form of the occasional ghost he speaks that I have substantiated in more recent times.

I have witnessed well over 1000 paranormal incidents, all in the company of others. In qualifying this there have been over 1000 experiences alone at the Haunted Tower on my tours over a seven-year period to 2021. Of the ghosts Linskill mentions, I have seen the White Lady numerous times in three locations, the nun once, and I heard the coach in 1982 in Market Street. Although these are the more well-known ghosts, there are a lot more besides. In his *Veiled Nun*, Linskill says, 'In fact, so numerous are they – 80 in number they seem to be – that there is really no room for any modem aspirants who may want a quiet place to appear and turn people's hair white.' I remember the days when I thought 80 was a lot!

Thus far, I have recorded over 300 ghosts in 198 haunted locations through 415 independent testimonial experiences. These are all in St Andrews from residents, students and visitors, plus shared experiences by myself with others. St Andrews is not a big place, yet I have found for its *size* to be the most haunted town in the world. A bold statement you may suppose, but nowhere else comes close.

As an aside, the most haunted building in the world is Glamis Castle in Angus, with over 90 individual entities. I am the only one to have researched Glamis and St Andrews for that matter to that degree of depth, which is how I know.

I have 7 present day reports of the (not so veiled) Nun of St Leonards, 31 for the White Lady, 13 for phantom monks (Square Tower), 2 for the floating head, 22 for phantom coaches/horses, 6 for dogs, leaving another 335 reports of incorporeal shades Linskill doesn't mention in his tales. There are 31 ghosts alone at St Leonards covering many more reports and Linskill picked up on 1 of them - the nun.

Other ghosts Linskill mentions such as the screaming skull are complete fiction, so too his description of the nun.

I have included a few experiential examples of his ghosts being observed through the text, either within introductions to a few of his stories or as footnotes.

The true extent of my involvement with Linskill and the full extent of the testimonies I have amassed, plus my correlation of the same, will all be found laced through my other St Andrews publications, especially *More Ghosts of St Andrews* (2021), with 612 pages it includes 314 new testimonial experiences and 260 new ghosts.

Cross-referencing

Some of Linskill's material changed through various editions, small details such as names were omitted, whole paragraphs altered, excluded or included. I have correlated all this where possible, and again added footnotes pertaining to variations of his stories appearing up to 1978. One prominent alteration concerns the term for a ghost he references ten times through his book. I mention this variance here for the sake of historical accuracy. He called the ghost of a black boy a 'nigger' which I have adjusted throughout this text to the term 'negro', which is the term adopted for his later editions.

As well as their being several variations to some of his stories in different editions, he also encompassed a whole host of paranormal activity into a few stories he had heard about but had no further information for other than their initial suggestion. The order of the stories also changed in later versions. I have adopted Linskill's original order barring *The Veiled Nun of St Leonards*, which now follows on from the two stories about the White Lady. I realised details in those stories tie directly in with elements of the Veiled Nun. My exploratory notes for this will be found after that story, along with a disclosure of Linskill's sources of inspiration for what is St Andrews most famous ghost story.

His book is not a long volume, latterly it only covered 87 pages, but he spent many years writing it and published various elements pre-1911. All comments in square brackets through the following and through his stories are my own.

Early work

As an example of Linskill's earlier published notes, some seven years before the publication of his booklet he wrote two short pieces for the *Fife Herald and Journal*, dated 13th and 27th January, 1904. The first is the introductory build up to what would become his story: *The Smothered Piper of the West Cliffs*, as follows:

Local Ghost Stories, St Andrews

'Some wonderful bogie stories ... of the ghost of Thomas Plater, who murdered Prior Robert of Montrose on the dormitory staircase before vespers: of the negro in a Fifeshire house, who is invisible himself[ii], but maps out his bare footmarks on the floor of the painted gallery [cf. Baft

_____

[ii] If the ghost was invisible why say it is a negro? What it doesn't say here is the ghost in question is of a negro servant boy who had also been seen as well as heard.

15

Barefoot, ante}:[iii] of [Archbishop] Sharp's [phantom] coach, which being heard, betokens a death; of haunted old Balcomie Castle; of the murdered pedlar in our own South Street, who sweeps down with a chilly hand the cheeks of invaders to his haunted cellar [Aikman and Terras, Bell Street]; of the ghost that appeared in the house of Archbishop Ross, mentioned in Lyon's History; and of the terrible ghost in the Novum Hospitium, which so alarmed the people that it had to be pulled down [1810]; and only a fragment now remains.'[iv]

The version in his book of 1911 then continues: '...but they wanted to hear the tale of the "Ghostly Piper of the West Cliffs"; so I told them the legend as I had heard it years ago....'

His second entry of 27th January 1904, with only a slight variation would be encompassed in his story *The True Tale of the Phantom Coach* of 1911 and read: 'The tale goes that the phantom coach finishes its nocturnal journey in the waves of St. Andrews Bay . . . [and] has been seen from time to time on the roads around St. Andrews.'[v]

Of the stories he mentions, it is interesting he gives preference to a couple of the more obscure hauntings such as Baff Barefoot or the murdered pedlar, the more famous ones make their appearance in *The Veiled Nun*.

Locations

Not all the stories are set in St Andrews. He included stories for other areas partly because he felt they were good ghost stories, and partly because (oddly) he didn't have as much for St Andrews as it might appear. Interestingly, he

---

[iii] Baft or Baff Barefoot is referring to the ghostly footsteps heard in Grangemuir Mansion House in Fife, which I recount in my book *Ghosts of Fife*, 2013.
[iv] Fife Herald and Journal, 13th January, 1904
[v] Fife Herald and Journal, 27th January, 1904

could easily have changed some location names to St Andrews and no one would have been any the wiser. Indeed, to switch this chain of thought about, I could equally say it is more than feasible for elements to be of St Andrews and he switched locations away from the town to preserve the integrity and privacy of those involved. There are moments where it is obvious he is referencing those he knew and who were still alive at the time, but a lot of his material remains obscure in this regard. His stories contain experiences through allegory, underlying themes and contexts still fresh in the minds of a few in 1911 and long lost to us now. Amongst the red herrings he frequently slips in, he does occasionally give clues to real locations and events. There is a story devoted to the fictitious Lausdree Castle near St Andrews for example. I have written an introduction for that story where I give details of the castle it was based on.

Characters

Playing on his antiquarian nature and the romantic ideals embedded in Victorian prose, Linskill brings the legends about the many ghosts to life through characters with humorous Dickensian styled names and nicknames. He partly took these from his Cambridge compatriots who would influence his ever-present tongue in cheek humour.

Captain Chester is a character who crops up throughout the book and is one of the few names without this flamboyant Dickensian flair. He certainly appeals to Linskill's alter ego and writes that he met Chester when he was an undergraduate at Cambridge University in September 1875. The same year he became a member of the R & A and the same year he founded the Cambridge University Golf Club. There is an idealism in the way Captain Chester carries himself through his many adventures, exploits and encounters. For example, the captain prefers to bag ghosts than exotic animals in some far-off jungle, which Linskill mentions he also did, and many Victorian gentleman of the day seemed to pride themselves on doing.

The Captain also refers to astral projection and other spiritual pursuits. These all fascinated Linskill, although you will note how he often downplays his belief in favour of a sceptical frame for his own character in his stories. Playing the devil's advocate to give contrast.

Pursuits

The Cathedral was a major hub of ecclesiastical life affecting the inhabitants, not only of St Andrews as a site of personal pilgrimage and worship, but of the surrounding lands as the ecclesiastical seat of Scotland. One commanding the Pope's brand of spiritual governance from its people. This all had a great effect on Linskill, who, so far as I can gather was of Catholic persuasion through his strong Irish roots.

He found St Andrews to be an ancient treasure filled with a trove of history, atmosphere and mystery. Shortly after the discovery of the subterranean passage at the Castle in 1879, he created the St Andrews Antiquarian Society to explore the possibility of this not being an isolated discovery. Right up to his death he strongly believed in the existence of subterranean passages under the town, and especially under the Cathedral precincts. A pursuit I have continued now for over forty years. In 1849, a spiral stone stair made of new white marble was discovered in the Cathedral precincts. It was seen by 18 people at the time and a drawing of it was made. It was almost immediately filled in with tons of rubbish. Capturing the imagination of an age, it became known as the 'Wee Stair'. As with all Linskill's labours and antiquarian pursuits he endeavoured to explore possibilities to their full. In the 1890s he gathered together those still alive to try and locate it. The precincts had changed so much in nearly 50 years and despite extensive digs, he never found it.

Linskill's Legacy

'Tommy' Linskill died peacefully at the age of 74 in 1929, and was buried in the family grave just north of the high altar of the Cathedral, near to where he believed the Wee Stair was located. In death, I feel sure he will have become acquainted with the deceased residents whose ghosts he often looked out for in the precincts, including the monk, and the White Lady of the Haunted Tower who he called his 'Juliet,' and the Wee Stair he spent exactly 50 years searching for.

Although Linskill is gradually being recognised as one of the early pioneers of golf, and his book on golf proved popular at the time, he is known more widely for his booklet *St Andrews Ghost Stories* in 1911. When it appeared on the shelves of the Citizen Office it made quite an impact. More so than he realised. Gaining momentum, his stories soon became engrained as legends resonating through the town as quickly as Dracula's exploits through a Transylvanian village. Filling homes with blood curdling tales, it has become somewhat of a classic around St Andrews. Published through J & G Innes and with thirteen editions, it was a local bestseller until 1978 when it went out of print. With his Victorian charm and charisma shining through his writing style, he captured the imagination of generations; from residents, students and visitors alike, with almost every household having leafed through its pages at one time or another.

As a flamboyant Victorian gentleman with a keen sense of humour and an even keener sense for golf and ghosts, Linskill would have quite a chuckle at the thought of his fictional stories having such a marked influence over 100 years after their publication. There are so many paranormal anomalies in St Andrews, it does get repetitive when his stories are brought out of retirement every time St Andrews and ghosts are mentioned on the internet, or dragged kicking and screaming around the time of Halloween into local newspaper articles. On saying that, why did I republish them? Linskill was my early inspiration and I felt it important to educate between the fact and the fiction of what he wrote; to fill in the gaps for a few stories, dispel a few myths along the way, and to give additional information pertinent to what he was writing. As it mentions on the back cover, I first republished his book as the back section of my *Ghosts of St Andrews* in 2013. Linskill's stories hold an important place in the psyche of St Andrews, and all the standalone copies appearing in recent years are poor quality online pod (print on demand) automated ocr scanned copies, churned out with jumbled words or missing text and generic covers that do Linskill, St Andrews and new generations to his work a grave injustice. They deserve more care than these could ever give credit, so, this is the first hand-transcribed copy since 1978, and certainly the first with annotations.

One thing is for sure, Linskill loved St Andrews and was renowned for knowing how to tell a ghostly yarn or two.

I finish this introduction of one of St Andrews enduring and endearing characters by saying as my own personal tribute – if one person were to haunt the old town of St Andrews it would surely be fitting if it were William Linskill.

If this is your first encounter with his work, then it is best you understand that Linskill left a few instructions for the reading of his stories. In-keeping with his desires, firstly be sure you have had a hearty meal in a congenial setting, then on retiring to your homely comforts, be sure it is dark, that the moon is full, and there is a suitably brewing storm to rattle the windows and chill the bones. Dim the lights or preferably switch them off and light a candle or a lantern, then once quite certain you are perfectly alone, sit back, relax, and enjoy St Andrews in the company of the Dean of Guild Linskill as your ever-present Victorian ghostly guide.

All the footnotes, additional introductions, photos and text in square brackets throughout the following are from Richard.

St Andrews

Ghost Stories

BY

W. T. LINSKILL
(Dean of Guild)

There are ghosts and phantoms round us,
On the mountains, on the sea;
Some are cold and some are clammy,
Some are hot as hot can be.
They can creep, and crawl, and hover,
And can howl, and shriek, and wail,
But those who want to hear of them
Must read this little tale.
W. T. L.

Published by
J. & G. Innes, *St. Andrews Citizen* Office.

———
1911 to 1978

This book on Bogies is dedicated to my old Friends,

John L. Low
(Laing)
and
Charles Blair MacDonald.

Note by Richard Falconer
The dedication for Charles appeared in a later edition then
both were dropped. So, who were his old friends?

John L. Low or John Laing Low was the
British Amateur Golf Championship
runner-up in the 1901 at the St Andrews
Links. Regarded as the greatest authority
on British Amateur Golf at the time, he
wrote several early books on the subject
and Captained the Cambridge
University Golf Club Linskill founded.

Charles Blair MacDonald
1855-1939

As a golfing architect, in 1893 he
designed the first 18-hole golf course
in the USA
(Chicago Golf Club)

Contents

	PAGE
The Beckoning Monk	29
The Hauntings and Mysteries of Lausdree Castle	38
A Haunted Manor House and the Duel at St. Andrews; or The Old Brown Witch	48
The Apparition of the Prior of Pittenweem	54
A True Tale of the Phantom Coach	62
The Monk of St. Rules Tower	67
Related by Captain Chester	72
The Screaming Skull of Greyfriars	77
The Spectre of the Castle	82
The Smothered Piper of the West Cliffs	88
The Beautiful White Lady of the Haunted Tower	92
Concerning more appearances of the White Lady	96
The Veiled Nun of St. Leonards	101
A Spiritualistic Séance	111
The Apparition of Sir Rodger De Wanklin	116
The Bewitched Ermentrude	121
A Very Peculiar House	127

Note on the Author

[This is not included in any scanned copy and was inserted as an obituary into the editions following his death in 1929.]

DEAN OF GUILD WILLIAM T. LINSKILL, the author of these ghost stories, was in his day one of the most interesting personalities of St. Andrews.

While not unmindful of the practical affairs of life, he specially delighted in wandering in the world of fancy. He had an intimate knowledge of the history of the city in which he made his home during the greatest part of his life, but it was its romantic legends that appealed most to him. He loved to depict in his numerous writings on St. Andrews the picturesque events of the ancient days, and he revelled in the telling of ghost stories, of which he had an unequalled collection. It was his natural style of telling these stories which gave them their chief charm. He related them as if entertaining a few friends seated in an old-fashioned inn puffing at their pipes with a cheering glass before them, while a log fire cast a mysterious light about the room.

One of the Dean's ambitions was to encounter a ghost himself, but in this he never succeeded, though he spent many eerie nights in houses supposed to be haunted. He gave as the reason of this failure, that he was not psychic.

The search for Underground St. Andrews by the "howkers" was to a large extent inspired by him [he was both the inspiration and the driving force]. He was convinced through his visits to the Catacombs of Rome and to the Cathedrals and other ecclesiastical buildings on the Continent that there must be an underground passage or passages connecting St. Andrews Cathedral with the old Castle or some of the former ecclesiastical buildings in the vicinity of the Cathedral. The discovery of the Subterranean passage at the Castle in 1879, when workmen were demolishing the old red-tiled cottage of the Keeper of the Castle, seemed to favour the theory of the existence of Underground St. Andrews, but no further discoveries of this nature have been made. [Not strictly true, but following his death in 1929, everyone would soon forget that for 50 years he commanded the enthusiasm of university professors and academics, the people of St Andrews and Scotland in his untiring search for what he and I know does exist.]

Dean of Guild Linskill – to use the designation he most preferred – was the son of Captain Linskill, Major of Tynemouth, and the Hon. Mrs Linskill. He was educated at Jesus College, Cambridge. When a youth his parents frequently brought him to St. Andrews to spend a holiday, and he took to golf so enthusiastically that in course of time he settled down in the Home of Golf.

Young Tom Morris was his golf tutor, and he played many rounds on the Old Course with this famous champion golfer.

The Dean was elected member of the Royal and Ancient Golf Club in 1875. He is still remembered as having introduced golf to Cambridge and founded the first golf club there.

A good all-round golfer, he excelled in putting. He was one of the earliest writers on how to play the game.

All his life the Dean was keenly interested in theatrics, and produced and acted in plays and pantomimes in St. Andrew. He also organised many concerts in aid of local charities.

For about a quarter of a century he served on St. Andrews Town Council and did much useful work for the city. He improved the lighting of the streets, was active in keeping the equipment of the Fire Brigade up-to-date, and during his term of office as Dean of Guild he gave good service in that department. He was as popular as a Town Councillor as he was as a citizen. In personal appearance the Dean, in later life, with his drooping moustache, portly figure, and stentorian voice, suggested retired Army Colonel, but he had no inclination towards warfare of any kind, and he exercised his voice in the singing of humorous songs, mostly original.

Mr H. V. Morton, the author of "In Search of Scotland," interviewed the Dean when he visited St. Andrews, and he has written of him that he had "one of the best memories I ever encountered," and that the Dean was "a great possession for any town and a still greater one for any publisher who could get a book out of him." This book of Ghost Stories has proved his most popular production.

But for the remarkable bit of good luck experienced by the Dean, St. Andrews would not have benefited by his long citizenship. He was a passenger in the ill-fated train which went to destruction with the fall of the Tay Bridge in December 1879. On that fateful night he was travelling from Edinburgh to St. Andrews and owing to the terrible storm which was raging, the cab which was to convey him from Leuchars to St. Andrews was delayed. He decided to proceed with the train to Dundee, and its wheels were in motion when the Stationmaster saw the cab coming and informed the Dean. Taking a boy who was accompanying him in his arms, the Dean jumped out of the train, and thus two lives were saved.

The Dean lived to be 74 years of age, his death taking place on 22nd November 1929. All St. Andrews regretted his passing.

A note by Richard

In my *Ghosts of Fife* (2013), I give a lot of detail for the Tay Bridge disaster, and thought it worth including the following photo here. This is the train that went down with the bridge. A haunting sight of itself. The train was salvaged, overhauled and put back into service in 1880. It then ran for another 39 years until 1919 and was nicknamed 'The Diver'!

From the Courier by Mr William M. Dow. December 1979: 'The final death toll was estimated at 75, but fewer than fifty bodies were recovered from the Tay. Passengers with season tickets or heading for destinations beyond Dundee were not accounted for. Similarly, children were not included in the tally. Because the total number of passengers was unknown, several local criminals, mostly wanted men, tried to take advantage of the situation. Witnesses were hired to state that these men had been seen boarding the train at various stations. As they were officially dead, the police were no longer looking for them and they were free to continue their criminal careers without interruption. This gave rise to the term "the ghost train" being used when referring to the train lost in the disaster. But many of the "ghosts" were still alive many years after!'

The Beckoning Monk

A brief introduction to Linskill's story by Richard

The *Beckoning Monk* in particular, can be likened to Linskill's own personal journey as he romanticises about what he longed to encounter, as if reminiscing upon his own past experiences. He imagined the monk to be guiding the unwary, including himself, through a labyrinth under the Cathedral where the secrets were to be found. Passageways inhabited by skeleton monks clothed in white (Culdee monks), and the famed White Lady (saint) who also makes a fleeting cameo appearance. With beautiful features and a long flowing white dress, he often searched the Cathedral grounds for her to no avail.

While St Andrews is no longer the political or spiritual seat of Scotland, when wandering through the old town, or rather, the old city, each corner turned reveals a new encounter with its spiritual, political and royal past. Just as Linskill's character in the *Beckoning Monk* becomes lost to his senses, St Andrews is so steeped in history it is easy to lose all sense of time when wandering its precincts. This is all part and parcel of the ways in which St Andrews imbues its own natural charm – and once experienced, its magnetism stays with the mind as it has done here since 500 BC.

The scene of the *Beckoning Monk* is complete with the sounds of chanting monks which were last heard in the siege tunnel of the Castle on two separate occasions as recently as 2014 by two completely separate visiting parties. The bells of the Cathedral ringing out in their once former glory are also given a mention. The latter is taken from a legend that when the Cathedral was ransacked in 1559, the bells were taken aboard a ship, which then sank in a storm in St Andrews Bay. The legend says the bells can still be heard to this day. They were last heard by a family visiting St Andrews from Saudi Arabia in 2017.

The Beckoning Monk

MANY years ago, about the time of the Tay Bridge gale, I was staying at Edinburgh with a friend of mine, an actor manager. I had just come down from the paint-room of the theatre, and was emerging from the stage-door, when I encountered Miss Elsie H ------, a then well-known actress.

"You are just the very person I wanted to meet," she said. "Allow me to introduce you to my friend, Mr Spencer Ashton.[6] He's not an actor, he's an artist, and he's got such a queer story about ghosts and things near your beloved St. Andrews."

Fred Vokes

I bowed to Mr Ashton, who was a quiet-looking man, pale and thin, rather like a benevolent animated hairpin. He reminded me somehow of *[Fred Vokes.]*[7] We shook hands warmly.

"Yes," he said, "my story sounds like fiction, but it is a fact, as I can prove. It is rather long, but it may possibly interest you. Where could we foregather?"

"Come and dine with me at the Edinburgh Hotel to-night at eight. I'll get a private room," I said.

"Right oh!" said he, and we parted.

---

[6] Spencer Ashton was an artist producing pastoral landscapes.
[7] Fred or Frederick was a famous Drury Lane Theatre actor and dancer. 1846 – 1888, which Linskill based this character on. His name isn't mentioned in some later editions of this book, being substituted simply as '*a friend*'.

That evening at eight o'clock we met at the old Edinburgh Hotel (now no longer in existence), and, after dinner, he told me his very remarkable tale.

"Some years ago," he said, "I was staying in a small coastal town in Fife, not very far from St. Andrews. I was painting some quaint houses and things of the sort that tickled my fancy at the time, and I was very much amused and excited by some of the bogie tales told me by the fisher folk. One story particularly interested me."

"And what was that?" I asked.

"Well, it was about a strange, dwarfish, old man, who, they swore, was constantly wandering about among the rocks at nightfall; a queer, uncanny creature they said, who was 'aye beckoning to them' and who was never seen or known in the daylight. I heard so much at various times and from various people about this old man that I resolved to look for him and see what his game really was. I went down to the beach times without number, but saw nothing worse than myself, and I was almost giving the job up as hopeless, when one night 'I struck oil,' as the Yankees would say."

"Good," I said, "let me hear."

"It was after dusk," he proceeded, "very rough and windy, but with a feeble moon peeping out at times between the racing clouds. I was alone on the beach. Next moment I was *not* alone."

"Not alone," I remarked, "Who was there?"

"Certainly not alone," said Ashton. "About three yards from me stood a quaint, short, shrivelled, old creature. At that time the comic opera of 'Pinafore'[8] was new to the stage-loving world, and this strange being resembled the character of 'Dick Deadeye' in that piece. But this old man was much uglier and more repulsive. He wore a tattered monk's robe, had a fringe of black hair, heavy black eyebrows, very protruding teeth, and a pale, pointed, unshaven chin.

---

[8] HMS Pinafore by Arthur Sullivan and W. S. Gilbert. May 1878. Some 18 months before the Tay Bridge disaster.

Moreover, he possessed only one eye, which was large and telescopic looking [penetrating].”

“What a horrible brute,” I said

“Oh! he wasn’t half so bad after all,” said Ashton, “though his appearance was certainly against him. He kept beckoning to me with a pale, withered hand, continually muttering, ‘Come.’ I felt compelled to follow him, and follow him I did.”

I lit up another pipe and listened intently.

“He took me,” resumed Ashton, “into a natural cave, a cleft in the rocks, and we went stumbling over the rocks and stones, and splashing into pools. At least I did. He seemed to get alone all right. At the far end of this clammy cave, a very narrow stair, cut out of solid rock, ascended abruptly about twenty or thirty steps, then turned a corner and descended again into a large passage. Then a mighty queer thing happened.”

“What might that be?” I enquired.

“Well, my guide somehow or other suddenly became possessed of a huge great candlestick with a lighted candle in it, about three feet high, which lit up the vaulted passage.

“ ‘We now stand in the monk’s sub-way,’ he said.

“ ‘Indeed, and who may you be? Are you a man or a ghost?’

“The queer figure turned, ‘I am human,’ he said, ‘do not fear me. I *was* a monk years ago, now I am reincarnate – time and space are nothing whatever to me. I only arrived a short while ago from Naples to meet you here.’

“Good heavens, Ashton,” I said, “is this all true?”

“Absolutely true, my dear fellow,” said Ashton. “I was in my sound senses, not hypnotised or anything of that sort, I assure you. On and on we went, the little man with his big candle leading the way, and I following. Two or three times the sub-way narrowed, and we had a tight squeeze to get through, I can tell you.”

“What a rum place,” I interjected.

"Yes, it was that," said Ashton, "but it got still rummer as we went up and down more stairs, and then popped through a hole into a lower gallery, and I noticed side passages branching off in several different directions.

" 'Walk carefully and look where you tread,' said my monkish guide. 'There are pitfalls here; be very wary.'

"Then I noticed at my feet a deep, rock-hewn pit about two feet wide right across the passage. 'What is that for?' I asked. 'To trap intruders and enemies,' said the little monk. '*Look down.*' I did so, and I saw at the bottom, in a pool of water, a whitened skull and a number of bones. We passed four or five such shafts in our progress."

"Upon my word, this beats me altogether," I interpolated.

"It would have beaten me altogether if I had fallen into one of those traps," said Ashton. "Suddenly the close, damp, fungus sort of air changed and I smelt a sweet fragrant odour. 'I smell incense,' I said to the monk.

" 'It is the wraith, or ghost, of a smell,' he said. 'There has been no incense hereaway since 1546[9]. There are ghosts of sounds and smells, just as there are ghosts of people. We are here surrounded by spirits, but they are transparent, and you cannot see them unless they are materialised, but you can feel them.'

" 'Hush, hark!' said the monk, and then I heard a muffled sound of most beautiful chiming bells, the like I had never heard before. " 'What is that?' I said.

" 'The old bells of St. Andrews Cathedral. That is the ghost of sounds long ago ceased,' and the monk muttered some Latin. Then all of a sudden I heard very beautiful chanting for a moment or more, then it died away.

---

[9] This is a reference to the siege of the Castle (Palace) of 29th May 1546, when the lairds of Fife (Castilians) murdered Cardinal Beaton and had control of the Castle. The Roman Church then set to work continuing a passage from a turret in the Castle perimeter wall to the Castle itself to gain entry or blow it up to get them out.

" 'That is the long dead choir of monks chanting vespers,' remarked my guide, sadly.

"At this moment the monk and I entered a large, rock-hewn chamber, wide and lofty. In it there were numerous huge old iron clamped chests of different sizes and shapes.

" 'These, said the monk, 'are packed full of treasures, jewels and vestments. They will be needed again someday. Above us *now* there are ploughed fields, but long ago right over our heads there existed a church and monastery to which these things belonged.' He pointed with a skinny claw of a hand to one corner of the chamber. 'There,' he said, 'is the stair that once led to the church above.'"

Ashton stopped and lit a cigar, then resumed.

"well, on we went again, turning, twisting, going up steps, round corners, through more holes, and stepping over pitfall shafts. It was a loathsome and gruesome place.

"Out of a side passage I saw a female figure glide quickly along. She was dressed as a bride for a wedding; then she disappeared.

"Fear not, said the monk, 'that is Mirren of Hepburn's Tower,[10] the White Lady. She can materialise herself and appear when she chooses, but she is not re-incarnate as I am.'

"Well, after we had gone on it seemed for hours, as I have described, the monk paused.

" 'I fear I must leave you,' he said, suddenly. 'I am wanted. Before I go, take this,' and he placed in my hand a tiny gold cup delicately chased; 'it is a talisman and will bring you good luck always,' he said. 'Keep it safe, I may never see you again here, but do not forget.'

"Then I was alone in black darkness. He and his candle had vanished in a second. Quite alone in that awful prison, heaven only knows how far below the ground, I could never

---

[10] His reference here is to Princess Mouren or Saint Mouren. She was a Pictish Princess of the Céilí Dé Pictish Royal Nunnery at Kirkheugh. Linskill references her again in *The Beautiful White Lady of the Haunted Tower*, p.92.

have gone back, and I feared to go forward. I was entombed in a worse place than the Roman Catacombs, with no hope of rescue, as it was unknown and forgotten by all."

"What a fearful position to be in," I said.

"I should think it was," said Ashton, "The awful horror of it I can never forget as long as I live. I was absolutely powerless and helpless. I had lost my nerve, and I screamed aloud in an agony of mind. I had some matches, and these I used at rare intervals, crawling carefully and feeling my way along the slimy floor of the passage. I had a terrible feeling, too, that something intangible, but horrible, was crawling along after me and stopping when I stopped. I heard it breathing. I struck a match, and it was lucky, for I just missed another of those pitfalls. By the light of the match I saw a small shrine in an alcove which had once been handsomely ornamented. My progress forward was suddenly stopped by a gruesome procession of skeleton monks all in white. They crossed the main sub-way from one side passage and entered another. Their heads were all grinning skulls, and in their long bony fingers they bore enormous candles, which illuminated the passage with a feeble blue glare."

"It's awful," I remarked.

"On, and on, I slowly went. It seemed hours and hours. I was exhausted and hungry and thirsty. After a time I passed through open oak and nail-studded doors that were rotting on their hinges, and then – *then*, I saw a *sight so horrible* that I would never mention it to anyone. I dare not, I may know its meaning someday – I hope so –"

"What on earth was it?" I inquired eagerly.

"For heaven's sake let me go on and do not ask about it," said Ashton, turning ghastly pale. "The horror of the whole thing so upset me that my foot slipped, and I fell down what seemed to be a steep stairway. As I struck the bottom I felt my left wrist snap, and I fainted. When I regained my senses for a brief moment, I found that the White Lady, bearing a taper, was bending kindly over me. She had a lovely face, but as pale as white marble. She laid an icy cold hand on my hot brow, and then all was darkness again.

"Now listen! Next time I came to myself and opened my eyes I was out of the accursed passage. I saw the sky and the stars, and I felt a fresh breeze blowing. Oh! Joy, I was back on the earth again, that I knew. I staggered feebly to my feet, and where on earth do you think I found I had been lying?"

"I cannot guess," I said.

"Just inside the archway of the Pends gateway at St. Andrews,"[11] said Ashton.

"How on earth did you get there?"

"Heaven knows," said Ashton. "I expect the White Lady helped me somehow. It all seemed like a fearful nightmare, but I had the gold cup in my pocket and my broken wrist to bear testimony to what I had gone through. To make a long story short, I went home to my people, where I lay for six long weeks suffering from brain fever and shock. I always carry the cup with me. I am not superstitious; but it brings me good luck *always*."

Ashton showed me the monk's gold cup. It was a beautiful little relic.

"Did you ever examine the place where you entered the passage?" I asked.

"Oh, yes," he replied, "I went there some years afterwards and found the cave, but it has all fallen in now."

"By Jove! It's very late, thanks for the dinner, I must be off. Good night."

I lit a pipe and pondered over that curious story. The entrance to the passage in the cave has fallen in; the exit from it in St. Andrews is unknown to Ashton – only the White Lady knows.

On the whole, the story is wrapped in mystery, and does not help one much to unravel the wonders that lie in underground St. Andrews. We may know some day or never.

---

[11] His reference here is to a tunnel he discovered at the Pends in 1894.

The Hauntings and Mysteries of Lausdree Castle

A brief introduction to Linskill's story by Richard

This next tale is all about Lausdree Castle near St Andrews. If you have read this story before you will realise there is a problem – or perhaps not so much a problem as a niggling in the back of the mind, which occurs a lot when reading Linskill's work. Lausdree Castle doesn't exist, and Linskill's story is primarily a work of fiction, yet I am sure many over the years have wondered if it could be based on an existing castle – and if this were the case, what castle might it be?

So, as an exercise, I thought I would see if there was a real Lausdree Castle. If there was somewhere close by that Linskill might have used as a partial inspiration for his story. Linskill's Lausdree Castle is Earlshall Castle near Leuchars.

He effectively states it in one of his stories supporting the theory of Earlshall as being an inspiration for Lausdree. At the start of '*The Spectre of the Castle*' he begins with a letter addressed to him as follows:

> Lausdree Castle,
> SIR, - Yours to command. Sir, I have not forgot our pleasant talk on that snowy night up in the far north, when you were pleased to be interested in my experiences of Lausdree. Could you very kindly meet me any day and time you choose to fix at Leuchars? And oblige. Your obedient servant,
> Jeremiah Anklebone

I have found Balgonie Castle south east of the Lomond Hills to be the most haunted castle in Fife, with 14 ghosts, but the ghostly associations there don't fit the bill nearly as closely.

It does give another angle to a story Linskill wrote as a piece of fictionalised fireside entertainment. On one level he didn't necessarily mean to be taken seriously, but having researched Linskill, he had a habit of masking truth in fiction, and he was subtle with his references or I guess inferences. A lot of them are too obscure to fathom. Some will be in-jokes for those he knew, others may have made complete sense at the time, but a century later their relevancy has faded.

There are occasional clues to his sources of inspiration, and these could well be shared between a mix of fiction and fact.

I have included a few correlations with Earlshall through the pages of the story. The ghosts of Earlshall are: a presence on the turret stairs, footsteps, something grabbing at the ankles when walking on the stair, the ghost of Sir Andrews Bruce, ghost of an old woman, ghost of a serving woman, blue lights and the indent of a body on a bed.

Further details of these ghosts can be found in my book *Ghosts of Fife* (2013).

Alongside the correlations with Earlshall, Linskill draws inspiration from Lordscairnie Castle, together with a South Street apparition and Ba'al, a well-known demon from the old grimoires.

Ba'al

The Hauntings and Mysteries of Lausdree Castle

It is many years ago since I was on a walking tour in the Highlands, far to the north of Bonnie Glenshee; and when on the moorlands I was overtaken for my sins, by a regular American snowstorm – a genuine blizzard of the most pronounced type. I struggled along as well as I could for some considerable time, and then I became aware that someone was beside me. It was a young Highland lassie with a plaid over her head. I was pleased to learn from her that her name was "Jean," that she was the niece of a neighbouring innkeeper, and that she would speedily convey me to his haven of rest. We trudged along in the blinding snow without a word, and I was more than thankful to the lassie when I at last found myself out of the snow in a nice little sanded parlour with a glorious fire of peat and logs blazing on the hospitable hearth. A glass of something hot, brought by mine host, was most welcome.

I found there was one other storm-stayed traveller in the wee house, an old family butler, whose name I discovered was Jeremiah Anklebone[12]. He had been on a visit to relations in the North, *[and had been caught in the snow like myself. We were both]* thankful to find such a warm, cosy shanty on such an inclement evening, and, to use a Scots term, we foregathered at the ingle inside.

He asked me if I knew much about spirits, to which I replied that I had just had a glass, but he at once explained

---

[12] As I mentioned in the introduction to this book regarding Linskill, he has a particular Dickensian touch when it comes to dishing out the humorous names. The name anklebone through this story is an inference to the ghost of 'Bloody' Bruce at Earlshall Castle, who it is said 'snatches at your ankle in the gloaming, as you go up or down the worn turret stair.' It is one of the most famous paranormal features of the castle and is too much of a coincidence that the butler of his fictitious castle was called Anklebone.

that although not averse to toddy, he alluded to spirits of another nature, viz., ghosts, banshees, boggards, and the like.

I told him I had frequently been in so-called haunted places in various countries, but had never seen or heard anything except owls, bats, rats, and mice.

He ventured the remark I had often heard before, that I could not be receptive, and I told him I was thankful that I was not.

He was a fine old fellow, an ideal family butler, and doubtless the recipient of many family secrets. He had big mutton-chop whiskers and a bald head, and looked as if he had served turtle soup all his life; but it was *not* soup he was soaked with – he seemed fairly saturated with spook lore. He informed me, quite calmly, that he was gifted with the remarkable faculty of seeing apparitions, demons, et cetera.

I could not help remarking that it seemed a very unpleasant faculty to possess, but he quite differed with me, and got as warm as his toddy on the subject, I shall not in a hurry forget that wild evening in the Highland inn before that blazing fire, or the wonderful narrations I heard from Butler Anklebone. Space precludes me from putting down here *all* the marvels he revealed to me.

It seemed all his life – he was 62 – he had been gasping like a fish on a river's bank to get into a really well-haunted house, but had utterly failed till he took the post of head butler at Lausdree Castle, which he informed me was but a short distance from St. Andrews. He gave me a most tremendous description of the old castle, and from his account it seemed to be the asylum and gathering place of *all* the bogies in Britain and elsewhere. Congregated together there were the Ice Maid, the Brown Lady, a headless man, a cauld lad, a black maiden, the Flaming Ghost, the Wandering Monk, a ghost called Silky[13], auld Martha, a radiant boy, an iron knight, a creeping ghost, jumping Jock, old No-legs, Great Eyes, a talking dog, the Corbie Craw, a

---

[13] Silky was a common name for 'imaginary friend's'.

floating head, a dead hand, bleeding footprints, and many other curious creatures far too numerous to mention.

The castle, he said, was full of uncouth and most peculiar sights and sounds, including rappings, hammerings, shrieks, groans, crashings, wailings, and the like.[14]

"What a remarkable place," I said to Mr Butler Anklebone, "and how do you account for so many spectres in so limited an area?"

"Oh! there is no time or space for them," he said, "they are earth-bound spirits, and can go from one part of the globe to another in a second; but they have their favourite haunts and meeting places just as we folks have, and Lausdree seems to appeal to their varied tastes."

He then went on to tell me some details of the Haunted Castle. "There are supposed to be," he said, "beneath the castle splendid old apartments, dungeons, winding passages, and cellars; but history states that any of those persons who tried to investigate these mysteries *returned no more*, so the entrances were walled up, and are now completely lost sight of.

"There is a built-up chamber, but no one durst open it, the penalty being total blindness or death, and such cases are on record. There is also a coffin room shaped exactly like its name; but one of the queerest places at Lausdree is a small apartment with a weird light of its own. At night this room

---

[14] I have found no associations for any of these apart from the wandering monk, which could be one of many, and the floating head which refers to 143 South Street built in 1800. His references to the other spectral visitations have all hallmarks of a classic fictional Victorian haunted Scottish Castle. They are also reminiscent of what he would have heard in passing in the Star Hotel. Indeed, the names and some of the ghosts are characters in-keeping with the tone of the nicknames and some characteristics of the regulars of the New Bar at that time, which then became the Star Bar. Linskill drew caricatures. One I have seen is a watercolour of regulars from the bar modelled on Punch and Judy and has a somewhat sinister quality.

can be seen from the old garden, showing a pale, uncanny, phosphorescent glow.[15]

"Mr Snaggers – that's the footman - and I unlocked the door and examined the place carefully. There was a table, a sofa, and a few old chairs therein, and an all-pervading sickly light equally diffused. The furniture throws no shadows whatever. The room seemed very chilly, and there was a feeling as if all one's vitality was being sucked out of one's body, and drawing one's breath caused pain. Snaggers felt the same. No one could live long in that eerie apartment. I know we were glad to lock it up again.

"Then there is a spiral stair, called 'Meg's Leg.' I don't know the legend, but almost every night one hears her leg stumping up these steps."[16]

"What a creepy place it must be, to be sure," I murmured, gravely.

"Yes!" said Anklebone, "and I tell you sir, Snaggers and I generally arranged to go up to bed together; one always felt there was something coming up the stairs behind one. When a person stopped, it stopped also, and one could hear it breathing and panting, but nothing was to be seen. Snaggers, one night when the candle went out, said he saw monstrous red eyes, but I saw nothing then. The creeping creature I only saw twice, it was like an enormous toad on spider's legs. They say it has a human head and face, but I only saw its back. [17] Some folks say it is alive and not a ghost, and that it

---

[15] At Earlshall, strange blue lights have been seen within the castle with no apparent source.

[16] Heavy footsteps have been heard on the spiral turret stairwell at Earlshall.

[17] He is describing the Demon Ba'al. One of the 7 Princes of Hell. Described in *Dictionnarie Infernal* by Collin de Plancy, 1818, as having three heads and spider's legs. The three heads are of a man, a toad and a cat. Linskill was an antiquarian and will have known this. This isn't the place to speak on such matters, but demons do have a reality and they are not the same as ghosts. They are the embodiment of very real forces, and have very a specific, sometimes singular remit: Ba'al - invisibility.

hides somewhere in the cellars, but we never could get a trace of it. One night I was going down to the service room when my way was barred by a ghastly, tall figure, with great holes where eyes should have been, so I just shut my eyes and rushed through it downstairs. When I got down, I found all my clothes were covered with a vile, sickly-smelling, sticky sort of oil, and I had to destroy them all."

"Go on, please," I said, "you astonish me vastly,"

"Yes," he said slowly, "It's all very queer. Lausdree is haunted and no mistake. Snaggers and I shared the same room. One night a great blood-stained hand and arm came round the corner of the bed curtain and tried to grab me. It was dead ice-cold too. Then a thing, an invisible thing, used to patter into the room, puffing and groaning, and get under the bed and heave it up, but we looked and there was never anything there, *[and the door locked too]*. We saw a great black corkscrew thing one night fall from the ceiling on to the floor and disappear, and then there was a mighty rush along the passage. Outside the door a great crash, a yell, and a groan dying away far below. There was a humorous spirit also, the Iron Knight. We called him 'Uncle.' He was up to tricks. We didn't mind him. When the fat cook was sitting down to a meal, he'd pull back her chair, and down she would come with a rare crash. If any of the maids upset a tray of tea-things, or fell downstairs with the kettle, or knocked over the great urn, they used to say – 'Oh! That's Uncle again!'"

I told him (Mr Anklebone) that I was delighted there was a touch of comedy in such a gruesome place, as I preferred comedians to ghosts any day. One thing I learnt from his story, and that was, that if he was head butler at Lausdree Castle, the head ghost was Sir Guy Ravelstocke, whose portrait still hung in the old picture gallery. The castle dated back to Norman times,[18] but about 1457 it fell into the hands

---

[18] While Earlshall Castle is not of Norman origin, the nearby Church of St. Athernase in Leuchars village dating back to the 12th century is of Norman origin.

of this Sir Guy Ravelstocke, who had been educated at the "Stadium Generale," or University of Saint Andrews. He and his two friends, Geoffrey De Beaumanoir and Roger Le Courville, held high revel and carnival in the old halls of Lausdree, and were the terror of the whole countryside. Sir Guy was a dissolute fellow, a gambler, and everything else bad. The neighbours alleged that he had sold himself to Old Nick.[19] He would spill blood as if it was water, and he and his white steed, "Nogo," were well known all over Fife and the Lothians. He was held to be a free-booter, a wizard and a warlock, a highwayman, a pirate, and a general desperado. He had slain many men in mortal combat, and was found invulnerable.[20]

"He must have been a sort of Michael Scott of Balwearie," I remarked.

"He must have been a holy terror," said the butler. "I've seen him often, exactly like his portrait in the picture gallery. I've seen him in his old-world dress with his sword hanging at his side, sometimes on his white horse and sometimes on foot.

"There were always terrible knockings, shrieks, and crashes before he appeared, and all our dogs showed the greatest terror. I slept in an old four-poster bed, and he used to draw aside the curtain and glare at me constantly. He nearly always was accompanied by the spectre of a negro carrying his head under his arm. Sir Guy was a great traveller in foreign lands, and, I have been told, used to bring back all sorts of curious animals and insects with him.[21] Perhaps that

---

[19] This is a reference to Earl Beardie of a different castle; Lordscairnie Castle whose legend has him playing cards with the Devil, and on losing the Devil takes his soul. Refer to *Ghosts of Fifes* (2013).

[20] Sir Guy Ravelstocke is quite possibly the 16th century Sir Andrew 'Bloody' Bruce of Earlshall.

[21] The Long Hall of Earlshall Castle was described by Russell Kirk in the 1950s as having a 'strange panelled hall with its painting of Princes and marvellous beasties.'

great toad thing I saw was one of the creatures. I've heard toads live for ages."

I said I believed that was quite true.

"I found a queer place one day," said Anklebone. "I was going up the turret staircase, and found some of the steps moved back. I got Mr Snaggers and Darkgood, the gardener, and we tugged them out. We called the master, and then we found narrow steps going down to a locked door. We forced it open, and got into a stone chamber. There were skulls and bones all over the place. Most of them belonged to animals, but there was a horrible thing on the floor, a sort of mummified vampire bat, with huge teeth and enormous outstretched wings, like thick parchment, and four legs. Perhaps it was a regular vampire. They fanned folks to sleep with their great wings, and then sucked their blood dry. We cleared out the room, and buried all the things in a wood.

"Now," said Anklebone, "I will tell you the end of Sir Guy Ravelstocke. He brought back with him from them foreign parts a negro servant, and they called him the 'Apostle'. Well, one night," he and his chums were dining, and full of wine, and the 'A – Postal' offended them somehow, and Sir Guy stabbed him. Then they chained his hands and feet together, took him to the dungeon, and filled his mouth, nose, and ears full of clay and left him. That is the negro ghost I saw always with Sir Guy – the murdered negro.

"About two years after, Sir Guy and his friends were in the same room drinking when there came a great hammering at the castle door. Sir Guy drew his sword, flung open the door, and plunged out into the darkness. A few moments passed then his friends rushed out on hearing wild unearthly shrieks, but there was no Sir Guy to be seen, he had totally disappeared, and was never heard of or seen in life again.[22]

---

[22] This again is a reference to Earl Beardie when the Devil first appeared to him in his castle and he reached for his sword. At the end of the night when he had lost at cards, the Devil had his soul and Earl Beardie disappeared from mortal gaze. A legend shared with Glamis.

We found his remains three years ago, but I will tell you of that directly. One day Snaggers and I had gone to St. Andrews to buy things. We were just at the end of South Street when a horseman dashed past us at full gallop. 'Heavens,' said Snaggers, 'it's Sir Guy as I live.' He went bang into the big iron gates at the Cathedral. When we came up the great gates were locked, and there was Sir Guy leaning up against the west gable scowling at us, but the white horse had gone, and he melted away as we looked. I saw him again with the negro at Magus Muir, and alone one dark night in North Street.

"I was alone one evening in the room below the banquet hall at Lausdree and heard a pattering on the table. On looking up I saw a stain in the ceiling, and drops of blood were dropping down on the table and the floor. The room above was the very place where the negro was stabbed. Next morning we went into the room where I saw the blood drip, and there was the mark of a bloody hand on the table, but no stain on the roof.

"Now for the discovery. I had often dreamed about an old overgrown well there was in the gardens, and felt very suspicious of what might be therein.[23] Then the gardener and the woodman told me they had frequently seen the awful spectre of Sir Guy and the 'Apostle' hovering round about the thicket that enclosed what was known as the haunted well, and then vanish in the brushwood without disturbing it. I felt sure that there lay the mystery of Sir Guy Ravelstocke. This idea was soon after confirmed by a curious occurrence. One morning Snaggers was dusting an old oil painting over the huge mantelpiece, and above the weeping stone in the great hall, when somehow or other he contrived to touch a secret spring and the painting flew back and revealed a chamber beyond.

---

[23] Earlshall Castle has an ancient well in the garden with a very elaborate iron well head.

"We sent for Master, and got down by some steps into the room. Such a queer place! It was octagonal in shape, and there had been either a great fire or an explosion there. The vaulted stone roof and floor were all blackened and cracked, and the fireplace and wood-panelling were all burnt and charred."

"Perhaps the chapel," I remarked.

"That is what Master said," replied the butler, "and there were remains of burnt tapestry, charred wood, and documents all over the stone floor. Master got one piece of burnt paper with faded writing on it in some foreign tongue. The odd thing was the big picture. The eyes were sort of convex like, and two holes were bored in the pupil of each of its eyes, so that anyone standing up on top of the stone stairs could see all that took place in the great hall below, and hear also.

"Master took the piece of parchment and managed to make out a few words. They were – 'I am sure that Ravelstocke lies in the old Prior's Well, with the dead negro servant we placed there. I would not go near that spot for my life. Heaven grant *it* may not come for me, I must leave the place.' That was all he could decipher on the burnt paper.

" 'We must explore that Prior's Well (evidently that is its name) tomorrow morning,' said our Master. We were all up at dawn, and got all the men available to cut down the shrubs, bushes, and the undergrowth round the well, the growth of ages. When the well was exposed it looked very like the holy well at St. Andrews[24], only it had been very finely carved and ornamented at one time. The entrance was a Norman archway, and the remains of an oak door still hung there. We found a shallow bath shaped pool of muddy water inside, and a lot of broken stones and bits of old statues and glass. At the far end was a large square opening a few feet above the pool of water. We, of course, made for this, and found there was a cell beyond. The whole wall on one side

---

[24] The Holy Well or St Leonards Well in the Eastern Cemetery.

was riven and rent, either by lightning or the effects of an earthquake shock. If that ancient well could have spoken it would have told us as queer tales as St Rule's Tower at St. Andrews.[25] There was a most curious, overpowering, sickening odour inside the place, like a vault or charnel house."

I remarked that I knew no smells worse than acetylene gas or the awful smell I unearthed when digging, long ago, opposite the St. Andrews Cathedral.[26]

"Well," said Anklebone, "I can't imagine a worse odour than there was beside that Prior's Well. It turned us all so faint. We had to get some brandy. We got into the far cell, and there were two skeleton bodies on the flagged floor. One was a blanched skeleton as far as the neck, but the skull was well preserved, and matted black hair still clung on it and round the jaw. All the teeth were in their place. Some rings had fallen from the bony fingers, and a sword, all eaten away by rust, lay beside the skeleton. The other was of a dark oak colour, the nails on the fingers and toes being quite perfect. Chains, also almost worn away, hung round the feet and hands.

" 'Good Heavens,' said Master, 'it is Sir Guy Ravelstocke and the murdered Apostle!' There was no doubt of that whatever. We had them removed and buried at once. The mystery was solved after all these long years.

"The negro had been placed there, but the mystery of Sir Guy was inexplicable. *Who came for him* that night when he rushed out of the door of Lausdree Castle, centuries ago, with his sword, and who carried him to his doom in the Prior's Well? No one can answer that terrible question now. Oh! that the old well could speak and reveal its secret."

---

[25] Referring to the murder of Robert De Montrose.
[26] When Linskill discovered an ancient latrine at the top of the Pends which he mistook for a subterranean passage. This is why present day academics don't take the existence of passages seriously - they should. An entrance to them will be found in a passage off one of these latrines.

A Haunted Manor House and the Duel at St. Andrews; or The Old Brown Witch.[27]

This can hardly be termed a St. Andrews ghost story, but it is so remarkably strange and weird that I have been specially requested to add it to the series, and there is an allusion to St Andrews in it after all.

Several years ago we had in the Golf Club at Cambridge a Russian Prince who took up golf, and the questions of spirits, bogies, witches, banshees, death warnings, and the like, equally strongly. He was a firm disbeliever in all of them, and belonged to a Phantasmalogical Research Society[28] to inquire into and expose all such things. I frequently have long letters from him from all sorts of remote parts of the world where he is investigating tales of haunted houses, churchyards, and so on; but from this, his last letter, he seems to have contrived to meet a *genuine* and very unpleasant sort of spectre. Of course I suppress all names.

"X------ x Manor,

Feb. -----, 1905.

Dear W. T. L., – Well, here I am, actually in a really haunted manor house at last, and I have had a most horribly, weird, and uncanny experience of a most loathsome appearance. I have been here a fortnight now – such a queer, great old house, all turrets and towers, and damp wings covered with ivy and creepers, and such small, narrow windows. It is on a slight elevation, and has in bygone days had a moat around it. It is surrounded by dense woods, and there is a black-looking lake at the back. The staircases are all stone and very narrow, and there is an old chapel and a

---

[27] In later editions, 'The Old Brown Witch' was dropped.
[28] The Society for Psychical Research

coffin room in the house. In the garden, in a yew avenue, is a vault and a tombstone, and thereby hangs my curious tale.

It seems that centuries ago a very unpleasant old widow lady, and a very unpleasant son, had the old house. She was a very ugly and eccentric creature, and a miser, and was nicknamed by the village folk "The Brown Witch." The tales about her on goings told to this day are most remarkable. It seems her son, who, according to all accounts, was a shocking bad lot, was killed in a duel, and the old lady died shortly afterwards a *raving maniac.*

She seems to have left a very curious will. I deal with only two details in it. One was that the chamber in which she lived and died was forever to be left *untouched and undisturbed*, but *unlocked*, or the disturber would be cursed with instant blindness and ultimately death. The second was that she was to be buried in the vault in the yew avenue that she had specially made for her remains; that she was to be dressed in her usual clothes and bonnet, and that she must be placed in a tightly-sealed *glass coffin*, so as to be visible to any intruder. My host told me the chamber or the vault in the grounds had never been interfered with, but that her appearances had been very frequent to most credible witnesses, and that such appearances all portended some dire calamity to someone.

She had appeared and terrified many visitors, both in the house and in the grounds. She had also been seen by the village pastor and by the servants. He had never seen her himself, but he had taken every measure he could think of to unravel the mystery, but in vain. The outdoor servants were terrified, and would never remain, and one lady visitor had been nearly driven mad by seeing her peering in at the window at dusk.

Of course, I laughed the tale to scorn, and also the story of the alarm bell which tolled at intervals without any apparent or human agency. Not even the bravest would dare to walk down the yew avenue after nightfall.

Well, I had been ten days in the house before anything happened. I must say, the wind and the rats, and owls and bats, and the tapping noise of the ivy on the old windows at night were rather creepy, but nothing really out of the common happened till the other night.

My room was in a long, narrow, old gallery. After cards and billiards, and at about 12.30, I was going off to my well-earned rest, and was getting near my door in the gallery, when I saw a faint light coming towards me round a corner. I went into my room and waited to see who was wandering about so late at night. Then a figure stopped at my door, evidently carrying a lighted old lantern. I raised my candle to have an inspection, and then, oh! horror! – I staggered back for a moment, for before me clearly stood the horrible figure of the old "Brown Witch," A cold sweat broke out all over me.

Far, far worse than the description. I saw her brown robe and the poke bonnet, the horrible face, the huge black sockets of the eyes without eyeballs, the nose gone, and, worst of all, that fearful grin, the cruel grin of a maniac, a wicked, terrible face.

I opened my drawer and seized my always loaded revolver. I shouted loudly, and fired *once, twice, thrice*. She never moved; only the horrible mocking smile grew wider and more devilish. I rushed forward, slammed my door to shut out the awful sight, and then collapsed back into a chair.

I must have hit it each time for certain. An offensive charnel house smell pervaded the air. Then the door flew open, and my host and several men and servants rushed into the room, anxiously asking what was the matter, and why I fired? I told them everything. We found the three bullet shots in the wall opposite my door. They *must* have passed through that abominable horror.

Need I say I spent a wretched night? In fact, I sat up and never went to bed at all. I resolved to leave next day early, but before doing that I determined at all hazards, to go into that vault and see what it contained, and also to carefully investigate the "Brown Witch's" chamber without disturbing anything in it. I told my host next day at breakfast what I proposed doing, and he offered no objection whatever, but declined absolutely to go near the vault or chamber himself, or to let any of his household do so.

"Oh! by-the-by, did you ring the alarm bell in the tower last night?" he asked me. "It was the sound of your shots and the great bell ringing immediately afterwards that brought me along so quickly to your room. We all heard it."

I told him I knew nothing of it and never even heard the bell.

"I thought that," he said, "for you were nearly off in a faint when we all came in and hardly knew us for a bit."

"I can't make out the bell," said my host, "or what on earth can make it ring so. It has no rope, and it cannot possibly be the wind. I must have it removed. Last time it rung loudly like that, my old housekeeper was found dead in her bed in the morning."

To make a long story short, the next thing I did was to get a couple of labourers to shovel away the earth and find the lid of the old vault in the yew avenue. This was soon done, and we quickly descended into the place with lights. We found ourselves in a large-built, clammy chamber, and on the floor lay a tattered and broken old lantern. At first we thought the chamber was empty, but all of a sudden we noticed a niche at one end and at once went forward to it. In this singular alcove was a large glass box, or coffin, standing on its end, and in it standing upright was the horrible eyeless mummy (still arrayed in the brown robe and poke bonnet) of the terrible creature I had seen in the gallery, and with the same mocking, grinning mouth and the huge ugly teeth. The same smell I have told you of before pervaded the whole place.

She was hermetically sealed up in this ghastly glass coffin and preserved. We were all very glad to leave that charnel-house and cover it up out of sight, but not out of memory. That would be perfectly impossible to any of us. I can't get that smell out of my nose yet. It would sicken you.

Next, I went to the chamber with a friend and my bicycle lantern to investigate. It was up a long, narrow stone stair. The old oak door (it was unlocked, as I said before) soon yielded to our combined efforts and creaked open, and we stood in a room of the Middle Ages. The old shutters were tightly closed. The ceiling, which had once been handsomely painted, was rapidly falling away and the tapestry was rotting off the walls. It had evidently once been a splendid apartment, but now it was given up to rats and moths and spiders and damp. It chilled one to the very marrow, and it had that same horrible smell. There was a four-poster bed in one corner with rags and shreds of curtains, probably where the old creature had died. The tables and chairs were covered with the dust of ages. There was no carpet of any kind. An old spinet stood against the wall; and papers were lying all over the place inches deep in dust. A few charred logs of wood lay in the gaping old fireplace with its old-time chimney corners, and there seemed to be bits of valuable old china and bric-a-brac about the place. Many pictures had fallen off the walls, but a few faded pencil drawings were still in their places. Just guess my surprise and astonishment when I found they were Scottish views – one of Edinburgh, one of Crail Church, and three of St. Andrews, including the old College and Chapel, the Castle, and St Leonards College, with date 1676. Here was another most curious thing I determined to ask about before I left. However, I touched nothing in the room, as I had promised my host, and besides – you will laugh – I had no wish to be stricken with the "Brown Witch's" promised curse of blindness and ultimate death to any intruder who touched her things. I dreaded her far too much since I had seen her in the gallery and in her tomb, and heard of her bewitched alarm bell, which portended death to someone.

Before I left, I mentioned the Scottish drawings in the witch's room to my host, and asked him if he could throw any light on how they came there.

Briefly, it seems that she (the witch) sent her son far away in those old days to a Scottish University, and St. Andrews was her choice. It seems he was very quarrelsome in his cups, and frequently fought duels, and generally proved the victor. One of the last he fought at Sauchope Stone, near Crail, with a nephew of the Laird of Balcomie Castle, and they fought with broadsword and buckler, and again the "Witch's" son killed his man. His last duel was fought on St. Andrews sands with rapiers, and he was run through the heart – a good job.

Now I must conclude. I am determined to investigate further the whole most mysterious affair. If you ever visit this place, my host, Mr -------, says he will let you explore the vault in the yew avenue, and see the coffin and the old witch, and you may also go and look at the chamber. If you ever do, take the advice of an old friend and do not *dare* to touch anything therein.

YOUR FRIEND TO COMMAND.

The Apparition of the Prior of Pittenweem

It was in September, 1875, that I first met dear old Captain Chester (now gone to his rest); and it was very many years before that date that he rented his fearsomely haunted old house in St. Andrews.

I was a Cambridge boy when I met him – how the undergraduates scorn that term "boy." He told me the following queer tales in the Poppledorf Avenue at Bonn when I was on holiday.

The house he rented at St. Andrews, from his accounts, must have been a most unpleasant and eerie dwelling. Rappings and hammerings were heard all over the house after nightfall, trembling of the walls, quiverings. Heavy falls and ear-piercing shrieks were also part of the nightly programme.

I suggested bats, rats, owls, and smugglers as the cause, which made the old man perfectly wild with rage, and caused him to use most unparliamentary language.

I pointed out that such language would probably have scared away any respectable ghost. However, let me tell the story in his own peculiar way.

"My brother and I took the house, sir," he said, "and we had a nephew and some nieces with us. There were also three middle-aged English servants at the time; and, gadsooth, sir, they had strange names. The cook possessed the extraordinary name of Maria Trombone, the housemaid was called Jemima Podge, and the other old cat was called Teresa Shadbolt.

"One evening I was sitting smoking in my study, when the door flew open with a bang and Maria rushed in.

" 'Zounds! Mrs Trombone,' I said, 'how dare you come into my room like this?'

" 'Well, sir,' she said, 'there are *hawful* things going on tonight. I'm *frighted* to death. I was washing hup, please sir, when something rushed passed me with a rustle, and I got a great smack on the cheek with a damp, cold hand, and then the place shook, and all the things clattered like anything.'

" 'Nonsense, Trombone,' I said, 'you were asleep, or have you been drinking, eh?'

" 'Lor' bless you, sir, no! never a drop; but last night, sir, Teresa Shadbolt had all the bedclothes pulled off her bed twice, sir, and Jane said a tall old man in a queer dressing-gown came into her room and brushed his white beard over her face, and, lor', sir, didn't you hear her a-screamin'?'

" 'No, I'm hanged if I did. You must all be stark, staring mad, you know.'

" 'Not a bit of us, master,' continued Mrs Trombone. 'There is something wrong about this blessed house – locked doors and windows fly wide open, and the bells keep ringin' at all hours of the night, and we hear steps on the stairs when everyone is in bed, and knocks, and crashes, and screams. Then the tables and things go moving about. No Christian could put up with it, please sir. *We must all leave.*'

"Well, I got all those women up, and they told me deuced queer things, but I squared them up at last."

"How?" I inquired.

"I doubled their wages, sir, and I told them they might all sleep in one room upstairs together, and I promised them a real good blow-out at Christmas, and so on.

"Next my nephew and little nieces saw the old man with the long white beard at various times in the passages and on the stairs. Oddly enough, my little nieces got quite accustomed to see the aged man with the grey beard, and were not a bit timid. They said he was just like the pictures of old Father Christmas, and he looked kind.

"I never saw him," continued Chester, "till one All Hallows Night, or Hallowe'en as they termed it in St. Andrews; but I will speak of that later on."

"Go on," I said, "it is very interesting indeed to me."

"The servants all saw him at times, and that old arch fiend, Trombone, was constantly getting frightened, and breaking things and fainting. I was myself annoyed by strange unearthly sounds when sitting smoking at night late. There were curious rollings and rumblings under the house, like enormous stone balls being bowled along, then a heavy thud followed by intolerable silence. Then there was a curious sound like muffled blinds being quickly drawn up and down; that and a sort of flapping and rustling seemed to pervade the air.

"This perplexed me, and I got in a detective; but he found out nothing at all. After much trouble and research I learned of the legend of the Prior of Pittenweem and his connection with the old house.

"It seems when Moray and his gang of plunderers shut up St Monance Church and the old Priory of Pittenweem, the last Prior (not Forman or Rowles), a very old man, was cut adrift, and for some months lay hidden at Newark Castle, food being brought him by some former monks. Newark Castle was burned, and this old Prior fled to Balcomie Castle. From there he went to Kinkell Cave near St Andrews."

"I know all those places well," I said.

"After some weeks, and when winter came, he took refuge in the very old house in which I lived. He seems to have been among both friends and foes there, and brawls were quite common things within those walls.

"One night those long dead and forgotten old-world inhabitants were startled from their slumbers by shots, the clashing of arms, and wild yells. To make a long tale short, that old Prior of Pittenweem was never seen by human eyes after that fearful night.

"Many suspected foul play, but in those times it was deemed best to keep one's mouth shut tight, and what mattered it if an old Prior disappeared?"

"They were awful times those," I said. "Glad we live in these days."

"Well, now," said the Captain, "I must come to the night of All Hallows E'en, or Holy Even, when the spirits of the night are said to wander abroad. We dined early in those days, and after dinner I walked down to an old Clubhouse in Golf Place, of which I was an hon. member, to play cards. It was a perfect night, and a few flakes of snow had begun to fall, and the wind was keen and sharp. When I left the Club later the ground was well covered with snow, but the storm had ceased, and the moon and stars were shining brightly in a clear sky. By Jove, sir, it was like fairyland, and all the church towers and house tops were glittering in the moonbeams.

"I wandered about the old place for fully an hour. It was lovely. I was reluctant to go indoors. Gad, sir, I got quite sad and poetical. I thought of my poor sister who died long ago and is buried in Stefano Rodundo at Rome, and lots of other things. Then I thought of St Andrews as it is and what it might have been. I thought of all its holy temples, erected by our pious forefathers, and its altars and statues lying desolate, ruined and profaned.

"At last I arrived at my own door, and entered – in a thoughtful mood. I went to my study and put on my slippers and dressing gown. I had just sat down and commenced reading when there came a most tremendous shivering crash. I involuntarily cowered down. I thought the roof had fallen – at least, gad, sir, I was flabbergasted. It woke everyone. The crash was followed by a roaring sound."

"It must have been an earthquake. Captain Chester," I said.

"Zounds, sir, I don't know what it was. I thought I was killed. Then my nephew and I got a lamp and examined the house.

"Everything was right – nothing to account for the fearful noise. Finally, we went downstairs to the vaulted kitchens. Zounds, sir, all of a sudden my nephew gripped my arm, and with a cry of abject terror pointed to the open kitchen door. 'Oh, look there, look there!' he almost screamed.

"I looked, and, gad, I got a queer turn. There facing us in the open doorway was a very tall, shaven-headed old man with a long grey beard. He had a white robe or cassock on, a linen rocket, and, above all, an almuce or cloak of black hue lined with ermine – *The Augustinian habit*. In one hand he held a very large rosary, and he lent on a stout cudgel.

"As I advanced he retreated backwards, always beckoning to me – and I followed lamp in hand. I *had* to follow – could not help myself. Do you know the way a serpent can fascinate or hypnotise its prey before it devours them?"

"Yes," I said, "I have seen the snakes at the Zoo do that trick."

"Well, sir, I was hypnotised like that – precisely like that. He beckoned and I followed.

Suddenly I saw a little door in the comer of the kitchen standing open – a door I had never noticed before. The shadowy vision backed towards it. Still I followed. Then he entered its portals. As I advanced he grew more and more transparent, and finally melted away, and the heavy door shut upon him with a tremendous crash and rattle. The lamp fell from my trembling hand and was shattered to fragments on the stone floor. I was in pitch darkness – silence reigned – I don't remember how I got out to the light again.

"Next morning early I got in some workmen and took them down to the kitchen, direct to the corner where the door was through which the apparition vanished the previous night.

"Zounds, sir, there was *no door there* – only the white plastered wall. I was dumfounded. 'Mrs Trombone,' I said to the cook, 'where the devil has that door gone?'"

" 'The door, sir,' said the cook, 'there ain't no door there that I ever saw.'

" 'Trombone,' I replied, 'don't tell falsehoods – you're a fool.'

"I made the men set to work and tear down the plaster and stuff, and, egad, sir, in an hour we found the door – a thick oak, nail studded, iron clamped old door. It took some time to force it open, and then down three steps we found ourselves in a chamber with mighty thick walls and with a flagged floor, about six feet square, lit by a small slit of a window.

" 'Tear up the flags,' I said.

"They did so, and there was only earth below.

" 'Dig down,' I said, 'dig like thunder,'

"In about an hour we came to a huge flag with a ring in it. Up it came, and below it was a dryly-built bottle-shaped well.

"We went down with lights. What do you think we found at the bottom of it?"

"Perhaps water," I suggested.

"Water be d------- ," said Captain Chester, "we found the mouldering skeleton of a very tall man in a sitting posture. Beside him lay a large rosary and a stout oak cudgel – the rosary and cudgel I had seen in the phantom's hands the previous night. My friend, I *had solved the problem* – that was the skeleton of the old Prior of Pittenweem who vanished in that house hundreds of years ago."

The True Tale of the Phantom Coach

A brief introduction to Linskill's story by Richard

I have 20 reports of the coach and or horses or a horse being heard and 2 reports of it being seen. It has been experienced both during the day and at night I have included a couple of reports below, including one from myself. The rest will all be found in my book *More Ghosts of St Andrews*, 2021.

The locations are as follows:

Strathkinness – St Andrews Road
Argyle Street
South Street
Market Street
Abbey Walk
The Pends Lane
Castle Sands
East Sands
St Andrews Bay (non-specific location)
Magus Moor (not Linskill)
Hepburn Garden's
Queen's Gardens
Church Street
North Street
South Castle Street

Other than the Strathkinness – St Andrews low road there are no reports of a coach and horses being heard on any of the other arteries into the town: St Andrews/Guardbridge Road, Largo Road, Crail Road, Anstruther Road or indeed the Grange Road. Typically, it is loud and fairly fast. The *instant* those hearing it and turn to the source it stops, and there is never anything that could have made the noise. The occurrence is always spontaneous and it always happens as an additional circumstance to our everyday lives. The majority experiencing it have never heard about the phenomenon here before. The last time it was heard in St Andrews was October 2020 by three visitors who were only here for a few hours and again knew nothing of a ghostly coach.

I heard the coach around 1 am in 1982. Myself and a friend John Briton shard a flat in the east end of Market Street. We were chatting away when we heard a coach. The sound was unmistakable as it trundled across the old cobbled stones, with the echoing sounds of several horse's hooves accompanied by heavy rattling chains making its way along Market Street. It was travelling east to west.

We looked at each other and few flew to the window to see what it was. The sound stopped as we did so and there was nothing to see. The street was as deserted as it ever was at that time of night.

I have included the following account recounted to me a few years ago by a couple whose testimony is not out of sync with the story written by Linskill you are about to read. It is also one of the more unusual.

It was by the village of Strathkinness at Magus Moor a few years ago when a couple walking through the woods one winter's morning saw the phantom coach. It was a cold, dry and crisp morning. The snow on the ground was about six inches deep. As they started walking through the snow across a clearing in a field by the woods of Magus Moor, they saw it. They were overtaken by a large black coach and four huge black horses travelling at high speed. It came from behind and really shook them up. They had no notification of its approach and the only sound was from their gasps as it passed. As it disappeared in the far trees it left no imprint in the snow. Their extraordinary experience has left its mark on them to this day.

The True Tale of the Phantom Coach

The great curtain had fallen after the pantomime, and I was standing chatting on the stage of the theatre at Cambridge when one of the stage men came to tell me I was wanted at the stage door and I must hurry up at once. Thither I proceeded, and found a lot of golfing boys, hunting boys, dramatic boys, who shouted out "Come along quick to the Blue Pig" (the "Blue Pig" is a Cambridge name for the Blue Boar Hotel), "We want you to meet a fellow called Willie Carson, and there is to be supper, and he has something to tell us. The 'Bogie Man' has gone on there now, so come right away."

THE LOUNGE, "BLUE BOAR HOTEL, CAMBRIDGE.

This postcard is the Lounge of the Blue Boar Hotel in Cambridge. The photo was taken at the turn of the twentieth century around the time Linskill visited the hotel and set the scene for his tale of the famed Phantom Coach!

Well off we went to the Blue Boar Hotel, and we found Carson sitting over a blazing fire, with a capital supper set in his nice old fashioned room, lit up with candles only, the picture of comfort – outside it was snowing hard and bitterly cold.

After a talk over merits of the pantomime, we did full justice to a most excellent supper, and then crowded round the blazing hearth to hear a story our host wanted to tell us.

"Did you ever hear of the Phantom Coach at St. Andrews?" he asked, turning to me suddenly and removing his cigar.

"Often," I replied, "I have heard most extraordinary yarns about it from lots of people; but why do you ask?"

"Because *I've seen it*," he replied, softly and thoughtfully. "Some five years ago. It was very, very strange, not to be forgotten and quite unexplainable; that is why I asked you here tonight. I wanted to talk to you about it." He stopped over the fire and was silent for a few minutes.

"Tell us all about it," we all shouted at once, "we won't make fun of it."

"There is nothing to make fun of; indeed, it's a true, solemn fact," he said. "Listen and I will try to tell you what I saw, but I can't half picture it properly. Five years ago I had just come home from America. I went to stay at St. Andrews for some golf. I think it was the latter half of August, and I must have been in the town about week at least, when one night – it was hot and stuffy, and about midnight – I determined to take a good long country walk, and struck out right along the road to Strathkinness.

"It was a hot, dark, and stormy night, not wet; fitful black clouds floated now and again at a rapid pace over the moon, which now and then shone out brightly; in the distance the sea made a perpetual moan, and at intervals the dark eastern sky was lit up by flashes of summer wildfire lighting over the distant Cathedral towers.

"Now and again I could hear the mutter of far-away thunder, and there were incessant gusts of wind. I must have been about two miles along the road, when I could discern some very large object approaching me rapidly. As it came nearer I noticed it resembled a coach, dark, heavy, primitive; it seemed to have four large black horses, and the driver was a muffled, shapeless figure. It approached with a low humming or buzzing sound, which was most peculiar and unpleasant to hear. The horses made a hollow kind of ticking sound with their feet, otherwise it was noiseless.

"No earthly coach of the kind could go without any ordinary sound. It was weird and eerie in the extreme. As it passed me the moon shone out brightly, and I saw for a second a ghastly white face at the coach window; but I saw those four strange, silent black horses, the more extraordinary, tall, swaddled-up shapeless driver, and the quaint black, gloomy old coach, with a coffin-shaped box on the roof, only far, far too well. One most remarkable thing was that it *threw no shadow* of any kind.

"Just as it passed me there was a terrific roar of thunder, and a blaze of lightning that nearly blinded me, and in the distance I saw that horrible ghastly receding coach; then clouds came over the moon and all was black – a darkness one could feel, a darkness of shut-up smothering vault. I felt sick and dazed for a minute or two. I could not make out if I had been struck by the lightning or was paralysed. However, after a bit it passed off; it was a horrible deathly feeling while it lasted. I never experienced a similar sensation before or since, and hope I never may again. *[Omitted from later editions - Another very curious thing was the behaviour of my collie dog, usually frightened at nothing, on the approach of the phantom (for phantom it was). He crouched down, shivering and whining, and as it drew nearer fled with a bark like a screech, and cowered down in the ditch at the roadside and gave forth low growls.]*

"I tell you, boys, it's all right in this room to talk about it, but none of you would have liked to be in my place that queer, uncanny night on that lonely road. That it was supernatural, I am convinced; it is a very thin veil between us and the unseen world of spirits.

"They say I possess a seventh sense, namely, second sight, and I know I shall never forget night's experience.

"But listen – the story is not ended yet. Next morning a telegram arrived from my brother in Kent, 'Are you alright?' I wondered much, and wired back that I was very well.

"The following day a letter came from my brother giving me a very curious explanation.

"The following afternoon of the day I saw the coach, my brother was looking out of one of the old manor house windows in Kent, when he and several others noticed a large bird, having most peculiar plumage, seated on the garden wall. No one had ever seen a bird of the kind before. He was rushing off for a gun to shoot it, when our father, who looked very white and scared, stopped him. 'Do not shoot,' he said, 'it would be of no use. That is the bird of ill omen to all our race, it only appears before a death. I have only once seen it before – that week your dear mother died.'

"My brother was so alarmed at this that he sent the wire I have mentioned to me at St. Andrews. By the next mail from Australia we learned that our eldest brother had died there the very day I saw the coach at St. Andrews and my brother saw the bird at our home in Kent. Very odd, is it not; but what do you know about that coach?

"Only tales," I said. "Many people swear they have heard it, or seen it, on stormy nights. I know a girl who swears to it, and also a doctor who passed it on the road, and it nearly frightened his horse to death and him too.

"The tale of the two tramps is funny. They were trudging into St. Andrews one wild stormy night when this uncanny coach overtook them. It stopped; the door opened, and a white hand beckoned towards them. One tramp rushed up and got in, then suddenly the door noiselessly shut and the coach moved off, leaving the other tramp alone in the pitiless wind and rain. 'I never saw my old mate again,' said the old man when he told the tale, 'and I never shall – that [*their*] old coach was nothing of this here world of ours, it took my old mate off to Davy Jones's locker mighty smart, poor fellow.'

"They say his body was found in the sea some months afterwards, and the tale goes that the phantom coach finishes its nocturnal journey in the waves of St. Andrews Bay."

"Whose coach is it?" asked all that were in the room.

"I cannot say; some say Bethune[29], others Sharpe[30], and others Hackston[31]; I do not know who is supposed to be the figure inside, unless it is his Satanic Majesty himself. At all events, it seems a certain fact that a phantom coach has been seen from time to time on the roads round St. Andrews. I have never seen any of these things myself."

"Well," said Carson, "that awful coach *does appear*; it appeared to me, and, doubtless, in the course of time will appear to many others. It bodes no one any good, and I pity with all my heart anyone who meets it. Beware of those roads late at night, or, like me, you may some day to your injury meet that ghastly, uncanny, old phantom coach. If so, you will remember it to your dying day."

"Curious thing that about seeing the coach and the bird at the same time, and in two places so far apart." Murmured the golfing Johnny, "and then Carson's brother dying too."

["I'd sooner see the bird than the coach," said one.

"Guess I'd rather not see either of them," said an American present, "glad we have no phantom coaches in Yankeeland."][32]

---

[29] Cardinal Beaton, murdered 1546 in the Castle.

[30] Archbishop Sharpe murdered 1679 at Magus Moor.

[31] David Hackston of Rathillet murdered 1680 at the Mercat Cross, Edinburgh.

[32] Only in the original story.

The Monk of St. Rule's Tower

Some years ago I was perfectly surrounded with crowds of bonny children in the St Albans Holborn district of London. I fancy they belonged to some guild or other, and they enacted the parts of imps, fairies, statues, &c., in various pantomimes in neighbouring theatres.

I had been invited there to amuse the kiddies with songs and imitations, and now they were all shrieking and yelling at the top of their voices for a ghost story. "It's getting near Christmas," they all shouted, "and we all want to hear about ghosts, real creepy ghosts." I pointed out the fact that most ghost stories were bunkum, and that such tales were very apt to keep wee laddies and lassies awake at night; but, bless you, they wouldn't listen to that one bit. They wanted ghosts, and ghosts they would have.

Well, in about an hour I had yarned off most of my best bogie stories. I had used up most of my tales regarding Scottish, English, and Continental castles, and the banshees, water kelpies, wraiths, &c., connected therewith; but still those children, like Oliver Twist, demanded more. I really was fairly stumped, when, all of a sudden, my mind flew back to 1875, when a strange story was told me by Captain Chester in the Coursal grounds at beautiful Baden-Baden. I first fell in with this dear old warrior in Rome, and we became firm friends, and travelled together for many cheery weeks. He told me his queer tale in the very strongest of military language, which I must omit. The language would be suitable to use in bunkers, but not on paper. It was a sultry day. So were his remarks.

It would seem that many years before, he had visited Scotland and England to try and see a ghost or two. He had been to Cumnor Hurst House in order to investigate the appearances of ill-fated Amy Robsart. He went to Rainham Hall to interview the famous Brown Lady, and he journeyed to Hampton Court to hear the Shrieking Ghost, and also went to Church Strelton to see if he could fix the ghost at the Copper Hole. In Scotland he followed the scent of various ghosts, and finally landed in St. Andrews.

"By Jove, sir," he said, "that's the place for ghosts. Every blessed corner is full of them – bang full. Look at those fellows in the castle dungeons, and Beaton and Sharpe and the men that got hanged and burned, and the old dev --– I mean witches.

I saw my ghost there. Years and years ago I took an old house in St. Andrews, which was a small place then. Very little golf was played, and there was very little to do. But, gad, sir, the ghosts were thick, and the quaint old bodies in the town were full of them. They could spin yarns for hours about phantom coaches, death knells, corpse candles, people going about in winding sheets, phantom hearses, and Lord knows what else. I loved it; it took me quite back to the middle ages."

So I told these children Captain Chester's tale, as nearly as possible in his own words, minus the forcible epithets. I managed to hit off his voice and manner, and this in particular seemed to amuse the bairns. "Egad, sir," he said, "it was a curious time. Of all the tales I heard, the one that pleased and fascinated me most was the legend of the monk that looks over St. Regulus's Tower on moonlight nights. I went thither every night, and constantly fancied I saw a figure peering over the edge, but was not certain. Then I got hold of a very old man, who related to me the old legend. It seems that years ago there was a good Prior of St. Andrews named Robert de Montrose. He ruled well, gently, and wisely, but among the monks there was one who was always in hot water, and whom Prior Robert had often to haul over the coals. He played practical jokes, often absented himself from the daily and nightly offices of Holy Kirk, and otherwise upset the rules and discipline. Finally, when Earl Douglas and his retinue came to St. Andrews to present to the Cathedral a costly statue, long known as the Douglas Lady, this monk made desperate love to one of the waiting women of Lady Douglas. For this he was imprisoned in the Priory Dungeon for some days. It was the custom of Robert de Montrose almost every fine night to ascend the tower of St Rule and admire the view. The summit was reached in those days by means of ladders and wooden landings – not, as it is now, by a stair. In those days, too, the apse and part of the nave were still standing, and the summit of the solemn old tower was crowned by a small spire. One evening just before Yuletide, when the Prior, as usual, was on the top of the tower, the contumacious monk slyly followed him up the ladders, stabbed him in the back with a small dagger, and flung him over the north side of the old tower."

"I thought, Captain Chester," I said, "that the murder took place on the Dormitory stairs."

"Gad, Zooks, and Oddbodkins, sir, I am telling you what I was told, and what I can prove, sir."

"All right," I replied, "please fire away."

"Well," continued Chester, "they told me the Prior had often been seen since peeping over the tower, and at times he was seen to fall, as he did years ago, from the summit. By the bye, his assassin was starved to death and buried in some old midden. One moonlight night as my brother and I were standing on the Kirkhill, to our horror and amazement we saw a figure appear suddenly on the top of the tower, leap on to the parapet, and deliberately jump over. Zounds, sir, my blood ran cold."

"We did not hesitate long, but jumped the low wall of the Cathedral. It was easily done in those days, and we were young and active, and hurried to the grim old tower. Just as we neared it, a monk passed us in the Augustinian habit, his cowl was thrown back, and for just one second we had a view of his pallid, handsome face and keen penetrating eyes. Then he disappeared as suddenly as he had appeared. We were alone in the moonlight, nothing stirring."

"That is very odd," I said.

"Zooks! sir, I have odder things still to tell you. We went home to the old house, had supper, and retired to bed thoughtfully. I woke about 2 a.m. The blinds were up and it was as clear as day with the moonlight. Imagine my blank astonishment when I clearly perceived, leaning up against the mantelpiece, the pallid monk I had seen a few hours before near the Square Tower. He leaned on his elbow and was gazing intently at me, while in his hand he held some object that had a blue glitter in the moonbeams.

"He smiled. 'Fear not, brother,' he said, 'I am Prior Robert of Montrose who quitted this earth many years syne, [33] and of whom you have been talking and thinking so much of late days. I saw you tonight in our cruelly ruined Abbey Kirk. Alas! alas! but I come from ayont[34] the distant hills and have far to go tonight.'

" 'What do you want, Holy Father?' I said, 'and what of your murder?'

" 'That is forgiven and forgotten long syne,' 'he said, 'and I love to revisit, *at times*, my old haunts, and so does he. You have in your regiment, methinks, one named Montrose, a scion of our family.'

" 'Yes,' I said, 'I know Bob Montrose well.'

" 'See you this dagger I hold,' said Prior Robert, 'it was with this I lost my life on this earth many years syne on the tower of blessed St Rule. They buried it with me in my stone kist; I will leave it here with you to give to my kinsman, for it will prove of use to him e'er he pass hence – mark my words.'

"He raised his hand as in act of blessing, and melted away. I fell back in a sleep or in a faint. When I woke the morning sun was streaming into my bedroom. At first I thought I had eaten too much supper and had a nightmare, but there on the table by my bed lay an old dagger of curious workmanship – the dagger that slew the Prior years and years

---

[33] Since
[34] Beyond

70

ago. I faithfully fulfilled my vow, and my friend, Major Bob Montrose, has now got his monkish ancestor's dagger."

"That's all Captain Chester told me, dear children. Goodbye, don't forget me, and do not forget old St. Andrews Ghosts, the Tower of St Rule, and the Spectre of Prior Robert of Montrose."

Then a modern hansom whirled me away to King's Cross.[35]

───────────────

[35] Figures have been seen at the top of the tower when all is locked up. Robert de Montrose was murdered in 1394 by Thomas Platter on the dormitory stair only yards from where he was buried. The lower stair where he fell still exists. Two days after Montrose was buried in the New Chapter House, Thomas Platter was brought forth and after a long discourse from Bishop Walter Trail to the clergy and people he was thrust bound into prison. Prison conditions were harsh and he too died soon after. His body was cast onto unhallowed ground or the 'dung hill'[35] as Lyon records in 1838, and I imagine quite accurately so.

Nothing more was heard of this incident until over '500 years later when an employee of one of the hotels in St Andrews had two visions, both connected with the above incident they were of a monk who appeared beside his bed. During the second visit the monk said he was Thomas Platter, who for his crime had fed on the bread of grief and the water of affliction till he died and his body cast onto unhallowed ground. As he had never received a Christian burial and the stonemason at work in the Priory had disturbed his remains, he entreated that his bones might now be interred with the rights of the Holy Church through the instrumentality of Lord Bute. So, on the 15th July 1898, the bones of Thomas Platter were exhumed. Carried by the visionary they were laid to rest in the consecrated grounds of the Cathedral. Also present at the re-burial were a local priest, Lord Bute and a prominent Benedictine monk who performed the last rights.' Wilkie, James, *Bygone Fife: From Culross to St. Andrews*, Blackwood; Edinburgh, 1931, pp.343-344. In an earlier report the visionary is described as a billiard marker. A lost profession for one who presided over billiard games in hotels and pubs. The council records state he was buried to the south of the St Rule's Tower.

Related by Captain Chester

In my travels I have met many extraordinary and remarkable people with hobbies and fads of various kinds, but I never met a man of such curious personality as this old friend of mine, Captain Chester. All his methods and ideas were purely original. Everyone has some hobby; his hobby was ghost and spook-hunting.

We were sitting one lovely September evening in the gardens of one of the hotels at Bonn, which stretched down to the river Rhine, listening to the band and watching the great rafts coming down the river from the Black Forest.

"By Jove, sir," said the old man, "I have shot big game in the Rockies, and hunted tigers and all that sort of thing; but, zooks! sir, I prefer hunting ghosts any day. That Robert de Montrose was the first I saw. There are shoals of these shades about, a perfect army of them everywhere, especially in St. Andrews. Gad, sir, you should hear the banshees shrieking at night in the Irish bogs. I don't believe in your infernal sea serpents, but I've seen water kelpies in the Scottish and American lakes."

I told him I had never heard a banshee or seen a water kelpie.

"Very likely, sir, very probable. Everyone can't see and hear these things. *I can.*"

I told him I had never seen a disembodied spirit, and didn't want to.

"Gad, zooks! sir, I consider disinspirited bodies far worse. They are quite common. I allude to human bodies that have lost their spirits or souls, and yet go about among us. Zounds! sir, my cousin is one of them."

"Ah," he continued, "detached personality is a curious thing. I can detach my personality, can you?"

"Most certainly not," I said, "what the deuce do you mean?"

"Mean," he said, "I mean my spirit can float out of my body at will. My spirit becomes a sort of mental balloon. I can then defy destiny."[36]

"How in thunder do you manage to do it anyway?"

"By practice, sir, of course. When my spirit floats out of my body, I can see my own old body sitting in my arm-chair and an ugly old wreck of a body it is. It is bad for one, I admit; it is very weakening. Another thing may happen; another wandering spirit may suddenly take possession of one's body, and then one's own spirit can't get back again, and it becomes a wandering spirit, and is always trying to force itself into other people's bodies. Then one's spirit gets into a mental bunker, you see."

"I don't see a bit. It is most unpleasant. Tell me about ghosts you have seen, and about that dagger you gave Major Montrose."

"Oh! so then you are not interested in eliminated personality?"

"Not a bit," I said, "I don't know what it is. Tell me about that dagger for a change."

"Oh! ah! Well, the dagger Robert of Montrose gave me proved of great use to my old friend. Bob Montrose, on *many* occasions. It had a wonderful power of its own. Once he got into a broil with a lot of Spanish fellows one night, and as he was unarmed at the time he was in a remarkably tight corner. Suddenly something slipped into his hand, and, by Jove, sir, it was the dagger, and that dagger saved his life. Another time he found himself in an American train with a raving lunatic, and if it had not been for the protecting dagger he'd have been torn limb from limb. After that he took it everywhere with him."

"Where is it now?"

---

[36] By this, Linskill through Chester is implying that with astral projection he is as he shall be in death – still aware and alive in spirit. Any who can employ astral projection will know this is true and not some psychological fancy.

"Well, there's an odd thing if you like. Bob died in the Isle of France, where Paul and Virginia used to be. He was killed by a fall, and is buried there. He left the dagger to me in his will, but no human eyes have ever seen that dagger since his death. It may have been stolen, or it may have gone back to where it came from into Robert of Montrose's stone kist in the old Chapter-House at St Andrews Cathedral. Probably its usefulness was at an end, and it was needed no more. Bob told me one queer thing about that dagger. *Once a year* near Christmastide (the dagger hung on the wall of his bedroom) it used to exude a thick reddish fluid like blood, which used to cover the blade in large drops, and it remained so for several hours – and, again, sometimes at night it used to shine with a bright light of its own."

"That is indeed wonderful," I said, lighting another cheroot, "but tell me more about the St Andrews bogles. Astral bodies, dual personality, and things of that kind depress me a bit."

"Well, that is odd," said old Chester, "I love them. When I was in St. Andrews I rented a fine old house, with huge thick walls, big fireplaces, funny corkscrew stairs, such rum holes and corners, and big vaulted kitchens. It's all pulled down now, I believe, and a brand new house built; but I hear the vaulted rooms below are left exactly as they were. People didn't take to the old house; they heard noises and rappings, and saw things in the night, and so on. *We all saw things.* My brother met the ghost of a horrible looking old witch, quite in the orthodox dress, on the Witch Hill above the Witch Lake. It upset him terribly at the time – made him quite ill – nerves went all to pot – would not sleep in a room by himself after that. He made me devilish angry, sir, I can tell you."

"Perhaps it was Mother Alison Craik, a well-known witch, who was burnt there."

"Likely enough, sir, it may have been the old cat you mention, an old hag. Then my nephew and I saw that phantom coach in the Abbey Walk one windy moonlit night.

It passed us very quickly." but made a deuced row, like a lifeboat carriage."

"What was it like?"

"Like a huge black box with windows in it, and a queer light inside. It reminded me of a great coffin. Ugly looking affair; very uncanny thing to meet at that time of night and in such a lonely spot. It was soon gone, but we heard its muffled rumbling noise for a long time."

"What were the horses like, eh?"

"Shadowy looking black things, like great black beetles with long thin legs."

"And what was the driver like?" I asked.

"He was a tall thin, black object also, like a big, black, lank lobster, with a cocked hat on the top. That's all I could see. On the top of the coach was an object that looked like a gigantic tarantula spider, with a head like a moving gargoyle. I can't get at the real history of that mysterious old coach yet. I don't believe it has anything whatever to do with the murdered prelates, Beaton or Sharpe. However, the coach does go about. Another wraith I saw at the Castle of St. Andrews was that of James Hepburn, Earl of Bothwell, third husband of Mary Queen of Scots. He lies buried in the crypt of Faarveile Church, close to the Cattegat. Before his death he was a prisoner at Malmo; then he was sent to Denmark, and died in the dungeon of the State prison at Drachsholm."

"I am awfully interested," I said, "about those times and in Bothwell and Mary in particular."

"Odd's fish, sir," said Chester, "so am I. I went to Faarveile to see Bothwell's well-preserved body. The verger took me down a trap-door near the altar, and there it lies in a lidless box, a very fine face, with a cynical and mocking mouth. He murdered Darnley, and he was treated and buried as a murderer in those bygone days. At Malmo folks say he was tormented by the ghosts of his mad wife, Jane Huntly, and by Darnley. He ended his days in misery, and serve him devilish well right, say I. I love and revere lovely

Mary Stuart. Damn it, sir, he deserted her when she was in a fix at Carberry Hill, the curmudgeon."

"But what of the appearances of the Earl you saw?"

"Met him twice at the castle – no mistaking him – a big, knightly, handsome fellow. Spirits can easily at times assume their earthly form and dress. I recognised him at once — the sneering lips and all, just like his pictures, too. When he glided past me his teeth were chattering like a dice-box, and the wind was whistling through his neck bones. I addressed him boldly by name, but he melted away. One sees these apparitions with one's mental eyes. I saw him again leaning against the door that leads to that oubliette in the Sea Tower of the castle.[37] Egad, sir, he *exactly* resembled the body I saw in the old crypt at Faarviele. He often appears there, and at Hermitage Castle also. No mistake, sir, that was Hepburn, the Earl of Bothwell. I must turn into bed now. I go to the service at the Cathedral here early tomorrow."

Then the tall figure of Captain Chester strode away and left me alone to my meditations.

Well! I suppose if *I had been* Captain Chester, left alone there in those gardens, I'd have seen a ghost or two with my mental eyes; but, instead, I saw a fat waiter approaching, who told me my supper awaited me.

---

[37] A description fitting that of Bothwell – or more the point, a figure wearing sixteenth century attire, has been seen at the Kitchen Tower looking out to sea and leaning against the wall by the Bottle Dungeon. There are at least six ghosts in the Castle.

The Screaming Skull of Greyfriars

I NEVER met a better fellow in the world than my old friend, Allan Beauchamp. He had been educated at Eton, and Magdalene at Oxford, after which he joined a crack regiment, and later on took it into his head to turn doctor. He was a great traveller and a magnificent athlete. There was no game in which he did not excel. Curiously enough, he hated music; he had no ear for it, and he did not know the difference between the airs of "Tommy, make room for your uncle" and "The Lost Chord." He was tremendously proud of his pedigree; he had descended from the de Beauchamps[38], and one of his ancestors, he gravely informed people, had helped Noah to get the wasps and elephants into the Ark. Another of them seems to have been not very far away in the Garden of Eden. In fact, they seem to have been quite prehistoric. He was quite cracked on the subject of brain transference, telepathy, spiritualism, ghosts, warnings, and the like, and on these points he was most uncanny and fearsome. The literature he had about them was blood curdling. He believed in dual personality, and in visions, horoscopes, and dreams. He showed me a pamphlet he had written, entitled "The Toad-faced Demon of Lone Devil's Dyke." He was always flitting about Britain exploring haunted houses and castles, and sleeping in haunted rooms when it was possible. Some years ago Beauchamp and myself, accompanied by his faithful valet, rejoicing in the name of Pellingham Truffles, went to the Highlands for a bit of quiet and rest, and it was there I heard his curious story of the skull.

We were sitting over a cosy fire after dinner. It was snowing hard outside, and very cold. Our pipes were alight and our grog on the table, when Allan Beauchamp suddenly

---

[38] The Beauchamp's are an ancient family originating in France before 1066 when the name was brought to England during the Norman conquest.

remarked – "It's a deuced curious thing for a man to be always followed about the place by a confounded grinning skull."

"Eh, what," I said, "who the deuce is being followed about by a skull? It's rubbish, and quite impossible."

"Not a bit," said my friend, "I've had a skull after me more or less for several years."

"It sounds like a remark a lunatic would make," I rejoined rather crossly. "Do not talk bunkum. You'll go dotty if you believe such infernal rot."

"It is not bunkum or rot a bit," said Allan, "It's gospel truth. Ask Truffles, ask Jack Weston, or Jimmy Darkgood, or any of my south country pals."

"I don't know Jack Weston or Jimmy Darkgood," I said, "but tell me the whole story, and some day, if it's good, I'll put it in the *St. Andrews Citizen*."

"It's mostly about St. Andrews," said Beauchamp, "so here goes, but shove on some coals first."

I did so, and then requested him to fire away.

"It was long, long ago, I think about the year 1513, that one of my ancestors, a man called Neville de Beauchamp, resided in Scotland. It seems he was an uncommonly wild dog, went in for racing and cards, and could take his wine and ale with any of them even in those hard-drinking days. He was known as Flash Neville. Later on he married a pretty girl, the daughter of a silk mercer in Perth, who, it seems, died (they said of a broken heart) two years later. Neville de Beauchamp was seized with awful remorse, and became shortly after a monk in Greyfriars Monastery at St. Andrews. After Neville's wife's death, her relations seem to have been on the hunt after him, burning for revenge, and the girl's brother, a rough, wild dog in those stormy days, at last managed to track his quarry down in the monastery at St. Andrews."

"Very interesting," I said, "that monastery stood very nearly on the site of the present infant school, and we found the well in 1880. Well, what did this brother do, eh?"

"It seems that one afternoon after vespers he forced his way into the Monastery Chapel, sought out Neville de Beauchamp, and slashed off his head with a sword in the aisle of the Kirk. Now a queer thing happened – his body fell on the floor, but the severed head, with a wild scream, flew up to the chapel ceiling and vanished through its roof."

"Mighty queer that," I said.

"The body was reverently buried," went on Allan, "but the head never was recovered, and, whirling through the air over the monastery, screaming and groaning most pitifully, it used to cause great terror to the monks and others o' nights. It was a well-known story, and few cared to venture in that locality after nightfall. The head soon became a skull, and since that time has always haunted some member of the house of Beauchamp. Now comes a strange thing. I went a few years ago and lived in rooms at St. Andrews for a change, and while there I heard of my uncle's death somewhere abroad. I had never seen him, but I had frequently heard that he was very much perplexed and worried by the tender attentions paid to him by the skull of Neville de Beauchamp, which was always turning up at odd times and in unexpected places."

"This is a grand tale," I said.

"Now I come on the job," said Allan, ruefully. "That uncle was the very last of our family, and I wondered if that skull would come my way. I felt very ill and nervous after I got the news of my uncle's death. A strange sense of depression and oppression overcame me, and I got very restless. One stormy evening I felt impelled by some strange influence to go out. I wandered about the place for several hours and got drenched. I felt as if I was walking in my sleep, or as if I had taken some drug or other. Then I had a sort of vision - I had just rounded the corner of North Bell Street."

"Now called Greyfriars Garden," I remarked.

"Yes! Well, when I got around that comer I saw a large, strange building before me. I opened a wicket gate and entered what I found to be the chapel; service was over, the lights were being extinguished, and the air was laden with incense. As I knelt in a corner of the chapel I saw the whole scene, the tragedy of which I had heard, enacted all over again. I saw that monk in the aisle, I saw a man rush in and cut off his head. I saw the body fall and the head fly up with a shriek to the roof. When I came to myself I found I was sitting on the low wall of the school.[39] I was very cold and wet, and I got up to go home. As I rose I saw lying on the pavement at my feet what appeared to be a small football. I gave it a vicious kick, when to my horror it turned over and I saw it was a skull. It was gnashing its teeth and moaning. Then with a shriek it flew up in the air and vanished. A horrible thing. Then I knew the worst. The skull of the monk Neville de Beauchamp had attached itself to me for life, I being the last of the race. Since then it is almost always with me."

"Where is it now?" I said, shuddering.

"Not very far away, you bet," he said.

"It's a most unpleasant tale," I said. "Good night, I'm off to bed after that"

I was in my first sleep about an hour afterwards, when a knock came to my door, and the valet came in.

"Sorry to disturb you, sir," he said, "but the skull has *just come back*. It's in the next room. Would you like to see it?"

"Certainly not," I roared. "Get away and let me go to sleep."

---

[39] This was Dr Bell's School for Infants, which became the West Infant School off St Mary's Place. Built in 1846, the school is now a council records building. The site of the former chapel was on the corner of St Marys Place and Greyfriars Garden, currently overgrown with bushes and what have suddenly become large trees! The Student's Union also occupies former Greyfriars monastery land.

Then and there I firmly resolved to leave next morning. I hated skulls, and I fancied that probably it might take a fancy to me, and I had no desire to be followed about the country by a skull as if it was a fox terrier.

Next morning I went in to breakfast. "Where is that beastly skull?" I said to Allan.

"Oh, it's off again somewhere. Heaven knows where; but I have had another vision, a waking vision."

"What was it?"

"Well," said Allan, "I saw the skull and a white hand which seemed to beckon to me beside it. Then they slowly receded and in their place was what looked like a big sheet of paper. On it in large letters were the words – *Your friend, Jack Weston, is dead.* This morning I got this wire telling me of his sudden death. Read it."

That afternoon I left the Highlands and Allan Beauchamp.

Since then I have constant letters from him from his home in England. He has tried every means possible to get rid of that monk's skull; but they are of no avail, it always returns. So he has made the best he can of it, and keeps it in a locked casket in an empty room at the end of a wing of the old house. He says it keeps fairly quiet, but on stormy nights wails and gruesome shrieks are heard from the casket in that closed apartment.

I heard from him last week. He said: -

"Dear W. T. L. – I don't think I mentioned that twice a year the skull of Neville de Beauchamp vanishes from its casket for a period of about two days. It is never away longer.

"I wonder if it still haunts its old monastery at St. Andrews where its owner was slain. Do write and tell me if anyone now in that vicinity hears or sees the screaming skull of my ancestor, Neville de Beauchamp."[40]

---

[40] There are at least two well attested ghosts of monks in the grounds, but there have never been any reports of a skull, shrieks or screams. Myself and staff of the Students Union have seen a monk in the union.

The Spectre of the Castle

Several years had elapsed since I met the butler of Lausdree Castle in the Highland Inn. I had just come up from the south of England for some golf and fresh air, and was looking over my letters one morning at breakfast when I opened the following missive: -

Lausdree Castle,

………..

SIR, - Yours to command. Sir, I have not forgot our pleasant talk on that snowy night up in the far north, when you were pleased to be interested in my experiences of Lausdree. Could you very kindly meet me any day and time you choose to fix at Leuchars? And oblige.

Your obedient servant,

JEREMIAH ANKLEBONE.

P.S. - I have something to divulge to you connected with St Andrews that may absorb your mind.

Accordingly, I fixed up arrangements and met Mr Anklebone at Leuchars, where we went to the nearest hostelry and ordered the best lunch they had there. Jeremiah looked thinner, older, and whiter than when I last saw him, doubtless owing to his frequent communing with spirits.

"How is Lausdree getting on?" I meekly inquired," and what of the ghosts?"

"It is getting on fine, sir. I have had a number of new experiences since I had the pleasure of seeing you last. You must understand, sir, that my family for generations have been favoured with occult powers. My father was a great seer, and my great-grandfather, Mr Concrikketty Anklebone, of the Isle of Skye, was a wonderful visionary."

Now, Anklebone was an interesting old fellow, but he had a tiresome habit of wandering away from his theme, and, as it were, getting off the main road into a labyrinth of bye - ways, and one had, metaphorically, to push him out of these side lanes and place him on his feet again in the main road.

"Before I come to St Andrews Castle," he said, "I must tell you about a queer episode of an astral body at Lausdree, a disentangled personality, as it were."

"Push along," I said, "and tell me."

"Well, one afternoon after luncheon the master and I were in the dining hall, when we saw a gentleman crossing the lawn towards the castle. He was a tall man in a riding dress, with curly hair and a large flowing moustache. He came up to the window and looked in earnestly at us, and then walked along the gravel-walk round to the castle door. 'Hullo!' said the master, 'that is my old friend, Jack Herbert, to whom I have let Lausdree for this summer. What on earth can bring him here? I'll go to the door myself and let him in. He never said he was coming.'

"In a minute or two the master came back looking bewildered. 'Anklebone,' he said, 'that's a *very* queer thing; there is nobody there! 'Perhaps,' I suggested, 'the gentleman has gone round to the stables'; so we both hurried off to look, but not a sign of anyone could be seen, and we stared blankly at each other. We could not make it out. Two days after, the master got a letter from Mr Jack Herbert telling him he had had a bad fall off his horse, had injured his spine, and was confined to bed.

"Mr Herbert went on to say that two days before, while he was asleep, he dreamt vividly that he was at Lausdree; that he crossed the lawn to the window of the dining hall, and, looking in, saw my master and the butler (that's me) in the room. He was going round to the front door when he awoke. Now that was his *astral body* that my Master and I saw. He loved Lausdree, and during sleep he came and paid us that visit. Queer, isn't it? Ten days after, he died. He wanted to see the old castle before he died, and his force of will power brought his double self, or astral body, to visit us. It is not so *uncommon* as people think.

"Numbers of people are seen in two places at once far apart. Look at Archbishop Sharpe of St Andrews. He was in Edinburgh, at Holyrood I think, and sent his servant over post haste to St. Andrews to bring back some papers he had forgotten there. When his trusty servant went up to his study in the Novum Hospitium to get the papers from the desk, lo! there was the Archbishop sitting in his usual chair and scowling at him. He told the Archbishop this when he returned with the papers to Edinburgh, but his Grace sternly bade him be silent and mention the matter to no one on pain of death.[41]

"Now, sir, it seems that my master is able to see astral bodies, for he saw Mr Jack Herbert, but I doubt if he could see a *real spirit*. Perhaps, sir," suggested Anklebone, politely, "you might be able to see astral bodies?"

"Thank you very much indeed," I replied, "but I'm ------ if I want to see anything of the sort; but I have heard a tale of an eminent man in London who took a nap in his armchair every afternoon, and while asleep appeared to his friends in different parts of the country, but I doubt the fact very much."

"Ah! "said the butler, very solemnly, "only about one in a thousand has the power of visualising real spirits. Many

---

[41] The word doppelganger is of German origin meaning; *look alike* or *double walker*. This part is true. It was recorded by Robert Wodrow 1679-1734, that Sharpe's footman saw the Bishop sitting at a table near the window. ' "Ho! My Lord! Well ridden indeed! I am sure I left you at Edinburgh at ten a – cloak, and yet you are here before me!..." The footman runs downstairs, and tells the Secretare or Chamberlane, that the Bishop was come home...' When they came back he had vanished. By all accounts the servants were looking under beds and in closets to find him. It is the earliest record of a doppelganger I have found.

ordinary persons have *long* sight, and some have *short* sight, but most people are short-sighted when ghosts are visible. The ghosts are really there all the time. Some people cannot see them, but can feel their presence or touch only. Most animals can see spirits; sometimes they are killed with terror when they see the spirits."

I pulled the bell rope and ordered some spirits for the butler.

"I don't think that will kill you with terror," I said when it arrived.

He looked grateful, and remarked that talking was dry work, however interesting the subject might be.

"Now, look here, Mr Anklebone," I said, "you know, I daresay, the stories about the Cathedral, the Haunted Tower, and all that. Please tell me what your experiences have been there."

Anklebone's whole appearance suddenly changed; he gripped my arm violently, shivered and shuddered, and turned ghastly pale. I thought he was going to have a fit.

"For pity's sake, sir," he said, trembling, "ask me nothing about that. There is something *too terrible* there, but I dare not reveal what I know and have seen to anyone. Do not allude to it again or it will drive me mad."

He lay back in his chair for a few moments with his eyes closed and shaking all over, but he gradually recovered his usual appearance.

"I wish to tell you about the castle Spectre," he said, weakly.

I must confess that I felt nonplussed and disappointed at the turn the conversation had taken, as whatever my private opinion was regarding the worthy Jeremiah's curious statements, still I felt anxious to find out his experiences at the Cathedral particularly. However, I swallowed my disappointment like a Trojan, and begged him to proceed.

He gulped down his spirits and informed me he felt better again, but he did not seem quite himself for some time.

"Well, sir," he said, "I often used to climb over the castle wall after dusk, and smoke my pipe and meditate on all the grand folk that must have been there in bygone days before the smash-up. I thought of lovely young Queen Mary, of Mary Hamilton, and her other Maries, of Lord Darnley, of the poet Castelar, of Lord Arran, and the Duke of Rothesay, and all the Stuart Kings that used to be there. Then I thought of Prior Hepburn and poor murdered Cardinal Beaton, and of monks, knights, and lovely wenches that used to frequent the old place. I loved it, for I have read history a lot. One could not help thinking of the feasting, revelry, and pageants of those interesting old times, and the grand services in the churches, and what fine dresses everybody wore."

I saw he was going bang off the subject again, and when he began to tell me there were lots of Anklebones in Norman times about Fifeshire, I had to pull him back with a jerk to his ghost at the castle.

"Very well, sir, I was in the castle one evening, and I was sitting on the parapet of the old wall when I saw a head appearing up the old broken steps on the east side of the castle that once led down to the great dining hall. I knew no one could now come up that way without a ladder from the sea beach, and when the figure got to the level ground it came right through the iron railing just as if obstruction were there. I stared hard and watched the advancing figure. It looked like a woman. I had heard of the Cardinal's ghost, and wondered if it could be his Eminence himself. Nearer and nearer it came, and although it was a gusty evening, I noticed the flowing garments of the approaching figure were quite still and unruffled by the wind. It was like a moving statue. As it passed me slowly a few yards away, I saw they were not the robes of a Cardinal, but those of an Archbishop. I am a Churchman, and know the garments quite well. I saw all his vestments clearly, and I shall never forget the pale, ashen set face, and the thin determined mouth. Then I noticed one *very very* strange thing - the statuesque tall figure had a thick rope round the neck, and the end of the rope was trailing along the grass behind it, but there was no sound whatever. On it went and began to climb the stairs to the upper apartments. I tried to follow, but could not move for a bit. I felt as if I was mesmerised or paralysed. I was all in a cold sweat, too, and I was glad to get away from the castle at last and hurry home. I haven't gone so fast for many years. When I went next day to Lausdree I made a clean breast of the whole affair to Master.

" 'Would you know him again?' he asked me.

" 'Aye,' I replied, 'I would know that face and figure among a thousand.'

" 'Come to the study,' said the master, 'and I will show you some pictures.'

"We went, and I looked over a number of them. At last I came to one that fairly transfixed me. There was no mistaking the face. Before me was the picture of the spectre I had seen the previous night in the ruined castle of Saint Andrews.

" 'Well, Anklebone,' said the master, 'this is *really wonderful,* and you actually saw the rope round the neck?'

" 'I did,' I said, 'as I am a living man, but who is it? It is not the Cardinal?'

" 'No,' said the master very gravely, *'this man* was publicly hanged by his enemies on a gibbet at the Market Cross of Stirling on April 1st, 1571.'

" 'But who was he?' I asked, imploringly.

" 'The man, or ghost, you saw,' said master, 'was Archbishop John Hamilton of St Andrews – in his own castle grounds where he once reigned supreme.'"

I said farewell to Mr Anklebone, and as I thought over his extraordinary story journeying home in the train, I could not help repeating over and over again to myself that very curious name that seemed to rhyme with the motion of the train - Concrikketty Anklebone.

The Smothered Piper of the West Cliffs

"Hush! hush! hush! Here comes the Bogie Man."

This was shouted out to me very loudly by a cheery golfing "Johnny," as I entered the merry smoking-room of the old 'Varsity Golf Club at Coldham Common, Cambridge, some years ago. "Draw in your arm-chair, light a cigar or a pipe, and tell us all [many celebrated actors were present] some of those wonderful bogie stories about dear St Andrews. It is the bogie time of the year, and you must remember I played the 'Bogie Man' for you in one of your big burlesques at St. Andrews and Cupar some years ago, so fire away with the bogies, please, and be quick."

Then I reeled off a big lot of yarns: of the ghost, Thomas Plater, who murdered Prior Robert of Montrose on the dormitory staircase before vespers; of the negro in a Fifeshire house, who is invisible himself, but maps out his bare footmarks on the floor of the painted gallery; of Sharpe's coach, which, being heard, betokens a death; of haunted old Balcomie ruined Castle; of the murdered pedlar in our own South Street, who sweeps down with a chilly hand the cheeks of invaders to his haunted cellar; of the ghost that appeared in the house of Archbishop Ross, mentioned in Lyon's History; and of the terrible ghost in the Novum Hospitium, which so alarmed people that its dwelling had to be pulled down [1810], and only a fragment of the building now remains [the arched entrance]. But they wanted to hear the tale of the "Ghostly Piper of the West Cliffs"; so I told them the legend as I had heard it years ago.

It seems that in the old days no houses existed on the Cliffs from the old Castle of Hamilton to the modern monument near the Witch Hill. It was all meadow land, much used for the grazing of cattle and sheep, and also much frequented as a playground for bygone children. On and over the face of the cliffs, slightly to the westward of Butts Wynd, existed then the entrance to a fearsome cave, or old ecclesiastical passage, which was a terror to many, and most people shunned it. It had many names, among them the "Jingling Cove," "The Jingling Man's Hole," "John's Coal Hole," and later "The Piper's Cave, or Grave." A few of the oldest inhabitants still remember it. A few knew a portion of it; none dared venture beyond this well-known portion. Like the interior of an old ice-house, it was dark, chilly, and clammy; its walls ran with cold sweat. It was partly natural, but mostly artificial - a most dark, creepy, and fearsome place.

In a description which I got of it many years ago, and which appeared in the *St Andrews Citizen*, I learn that "the opening of this cliff passage was small and triangular; it was situated on a projecting ledge of rock, and it was high enough, after entering, to enable a full-sized man to stand upright. From the opening it was a steep incline down for a distance of 49 feet, thereafter it proceeded in a level direction for over 70 feet, when it descended into a chamber. At the further end of this chamber were two, if not more, passages branching off from it. Between the passages was cut out in the rock a Latin cross." This would seem to point to an ecclesiastical connection, and had nothing whatever to do with the more modem smugglers' cave near the ladies' bathing place.

But enough of description. In bygone days, in a small cottage, little better than a hovel, situated in Argyle, lived an old dame named Goodman. She occupied one room, and her son and his young wife tenanted the other little chamber. He was a merry, dare-devil, happy-go-lucky lad, and he was famed as one of the best players on the bagpipes in all Fife; he would have pleased even Maggie Lauder[42]. Of nights at all hours he would make the old grass-grown streets lively

---

[42] Maggie Lauder is attributed to an ancient anonymous Scottish folk song about a Fife maiden and her meeting with Rob the Ranter, the best piper she had heard play in all of Fife.

with his music. "Jock the Piper," was a favourite among both young and old. He was much interested in the tale of the old West Cliff cave, and took a bet on with some cronies that on a New Year's night he would investigate the mysteries of the place, and play his pipes up it as far as he could go. His old mother, his wife, and many of his friends tried hard to dissuade him from doing so foolish and so foolhardy a thing; but he remained obdurate, and firmly stuck to his bet. On a dark New Year's night he started up the mysterious cavern with his pipes playing merrily; and they were heard, it is said, passing beneath Market Street, then they died away. They suddenly ceased, and were never more heard. He and his well-known pipes were never seen again.

Somewhere beneath St. Andrews lies the whitened bones of that by-gone piper lad, with his famous pipes beside him. Attempts were made to find him, but without avail; no one, not even the bravest, dared to venture into that passage full of damp foul air. His mother and wife were distracted, and the young wife used to sit for hours at the mouth of that death - trap cave. Finally, her mind gave way, and she used to wander at all hours down to the mouth of the cave where her husband had vanished. The following New Year's night she left the little cottage in Argyle, and putting a shawl over her wasted shoulders, turned to the old woman and said, "I'm going to my Jock" Morning came, but she never returned home. She had, indeed, gone to her lost "Jock." For years after, the small crouching figure of a woman could be seen on moonlight nights perched on the rock balcony of the fatal cave, dim, shadowy, and transparent. Wild shrieks and sounds of weird pipe music were constantly heard coming from out of that entrance.

In after years, when the houses were built, the mouth of this place was either built or covered up, and its memory only remains to us.

But what of "Piper Jock?" He, it is said, still walks the edge of the old cliffs; and his presence is heralded by an icy breath of cold air, and ill be it for anyone who meets or sees his phantom form or hears his pipe music. He seems to have the same effect as the ghost of "Nell Cook" in the dark entry at Canterbury, mentioned in the "Ingoldsby Legends," from which I must quote a few verses –

"And tho' two hundred years have flown,
Nell Cook doth still pursue
Her weary walk, and they who cross her path
The deed may rue.

Her fatal breath is fell as death!
The simoon's blast is not
More dire (a wind in Africa
That blows uncommon hot).

But all unlike the simoon's blast,
Her breath is deadly cold,
Delivering quivering, shivering shocks
Upon both young and old.

And whoso in the entry dark
Doth feel that fatal breath,
He ever dies within the year
Some dire untimely death."

So it is with him who meets "Piper Jock."

"By Jove," interrupted the golfing "Johnny," "has anyone seen him lately?"

"I only know of one man," I said, "who told me that one awful night in a heavy thunderstorm he had heard wild pipe music, and seen the figure of a curiously dressed piper walking along the cliff edge, *where no mortal could walk*, at a furious speed."

"What do you think of it all?" asked my golfing friend.

"I don't know, I'm sure; I am not receptive and don't see ghosts, but if I could only find now the mouth of that place, I bet another 'Jock' and I would get along it and find out the whereabouts of 'Jock the Piper' and his poor little wife. Here is my hansom. Good night, don't forget the Piper."

And they haven't.

The Beautiful White Lady
of the Haunted Tower

"How very, very lovely she was to be sure!"

"Of whom are you speaking?" I asked. "Of some of the Orchid or Veronique people, or of some of your own company? I did not know you were hard hit old chap." I was sitting in the smoking-room of the Great Northern Hotel, King's Cross, talking to an old friend, an Oxford man, but now the manager of a big theatrical company, when he suddenly made the above remark.

"No, no! Of none of those people," he replied; "but our talking of St. Andrews reminded me of a ghost, a phantom, or a spectre - call it what you choose - I saw in that ancient city several years ago - no horrid bogie, but a very lovely girl, indeed."

"By Jove," I said, "tell me about it; I want a new ghost tale very badly indeed. I know a lot of them, but perhaps this is something new and spicy."

"I am sure I do not know if it be new," he replied. "I have never seen anything spectral before or since, but I saw that lovely woman three different times. It must be fully ten years ago. I saw her twice on the Scores and once in an old house."

"Well, I must really hear all about it," I said. "Please fire away."

"All right, all right!" he said. "Now for her *first* appearance. I was living in St. Andrews at the time. It must have been the end of January or beginning of February, and I was strolling along to the Kirkhill after dinner and enjoying the fine evening and the keen sea breeze, and thinking about the old, old days of the Castle and Cathedral, of Beaton's ghost, and many other queer tales, when a female figure glided past me. She was in a long, flowing white dress, and had her beautiful dark hair hanging down past her waist. I was very much astonished to see a girl dressed in such a manner wandering about alone at such an hour, and I followed her along for several yards, when lo! just after she had passed the turret light she completely vanished near the square tower, which I was afterwards informed was known as the 'Haunted Tower,' I hunted all round the place carefully, but saw nothing more that night. Queer, wasn't it?"

"Certainly it was," I remarked; "but I know dozens of weird stories connected with that old tower. But what more have you to tell me?"

"Well," he continued, "as you may imagine, the whole affair worried and puzzled me considerably, but it was gradually vanishing from my mind when near the same place I saw her again. I had my sister with me this time, and we both can swear to it. It was a lovely night with a faint moon, and as the white lady swept past quite silently we saw the soft trailing dress and the long, black wavy hair. There was something like a rosary hanging from her waist, and a cross or a locket hanging round her throat.[43] As she passed she turned her head towards us, and we both noticed her beautiful features, especially her brilliant eyes. She vanished, as before, near that old tower. My sister was so awfully frightened that I had to hurry her off home. We were both absolutely convinced we had seen a being not of this world — a face never to be forgotten."

"How strange," I said. "You know, several people saw a girl in that built-up old turret lying in her coffin. A former priest of the Episcopal Church[44] here saw some masons repairing the wall of that tower, and their chisel fell into the turret through a chink. On removing a stone, they came upon a chamber within, and they saw a girl dressed in white, with long hair, lying in a coffin, wanting the lid. The hole was built up again at once. I know, and have often talked to

---

[43] Don't be duped by Linskill's description. The rosary, cross or a locket is a piece of romantic fiction that has tripped up many over the years.
[44] This was Rev. Skinner. The incident refers to 1860 or before.

persons who saw her there[45]. One of them was a mason employed at the work. The doorway of the tower is opened up now, and a grill put in, but there is no sign of the girl. Queer stories arose. Some said it was the remains of Princess Muren, daughter of Constantine.[46] Others said it was the embalmed body of some sweet girl Saint concealed there in times of trouble, and so on; but finish your story."

"I have little more to tell," he answered. "Some months afterwards I was a guest in an old house in Fifeshire, and was given the turret room. On the second night I went to bed early, as I had been at golf all day and felt awfully dead beat. I must have fallen asleep suddenly, as I left my candle burning on the table. All of a sudden I woke up with a start to find the now familiar figure of the "White Lady" at the foot of my bed. She was gazing at me intently. When I sat up she glided away behind the screen at the door. I jumped up, put on my dressing-gown, seized the candle, and made for the door. The lady was gone, and the door was as I left it when I went to bed — locked. I unlocked it, flung it open, and looked into the passage. There she was. I saw the white dress, the splendid hair, the rosary, and the gold locket quite plainly. She turned her lovely face to me and smiled a sweet, pathetic smile; gently raised her hand, and floated away towards the picture gallery. Now for the end. Next day my kind hostess took me through the old gallery. I saw pictures of all ages, sorts, and sizes; but imagine my amazement when I saw 'The White Lady' - the same white dress, the lovely sweet face and splendid eyes, the rosary, and a locket, which I now saw had on it the arms of Queen Mary and Lord Darnley. 'Who on earth is that?' I asked.

" 'You seem interested in that painting,' said Mrs ---.

"Well, that is a portrait of one of the lovely Mary Stuart's Maries. She was madly in love with Castelar, the French

---

[45] Stonemasons John Grieve and John Ainslie with Jesse Hall - local inspector of the Board of Works.
[46] On this he is quite correct.

minstrel, and after he was beheaded at St Andrews[47] she became a nun, and it is said died of grief in her nunnery."

"That is all, old boy," he said, "and it is late. I think it seems right; *that* girl I and my sister saw *must* have been the spirit of Marie --- ;[48] and perhaps it was she who was the occupant of that haunted tower - who knows? but I shall never, never see such a divinely beautiful face on this earth again."

---

[47] This was Pierre de Bocosel de Chastelard, a French poet, romantic, and all-round light-hearted companion of Mary Queen of Scots. Refer to the next footnote.

[48] The fictional Mary Hamilton he gives mention to in the next story.

Concerning More Appearances of the White Lady

I HAD been invited, and was sitting at tea with a very dear old lady friend of mine not long ago. It may seem strange, but tea is, I consider, an extra and an unnecessary meal. It does not appeal to me in the least, and only spoils one's dinner and digestion. The reason I went to tea was because in her note to me the lady mentioned that she had read my book of ghost tales, and that she was interested in ghosts in general and St. Andrews ghosts in particular, and that she knew lots of such stories in the days of her girlhood in St Andrews, now about 85 years ago. That is why I went to eat cakes with sugar, hot buttered toast, and drink tea as black as senna or a black draught. She had also informed me in the note that she could tell me a lot about the Haunted Tower and the Beautiful White Lady.

It took some time to get her to that point. She would talk about Archbishop Sharpe and his haunted house in the Pends Road, of the ghost seen by Archbishop Ross, of my friend the Veiled Nun, of the Cathedral and Mr John Knox, of Hungus, King of the Picts, of Constantine, Thomas Plater, and various others. She told me a long tale of the Rainham Ghost in Norfolk, known as "The Brown Lady of Rainham," whom her father Captain Marryat both saw, and so on.

At last we got near the subject I wished information on.

"In my young days," she said, "St Andrews was quite a wee bit place with grass-grown streets, red-tiled houses, outside stairs, queer narrow wynds, not over clean, only a few lights at night - here and there, an old bowet or oil lamp hanging at street corners. Everyone believed in Sharpe's Phantom Coach in those good old days."

"Did you ever see it?" I queried.

"No," she said, "but I have heard it rumble past, and I know those who have seen it, and many other things too."

"But tell me about the White Lady, please," I said.

"I will. Few people in those days cared to pass that haunted tower after nightfall. If they did they ran past it and also the castle. Those new-fangled incandescent gas lamps have spoiled it all now.[49] The White Lady was one of the *Maries*, one of the maids of honour to poor martyred Mary of Scotland, they said then. She was madly in love with the French poet and minstrel, 'Castelar,' and he was hopelessly in love, like many others, with Marie's lovely mistress, 'the Queen of Scots.'"

"Was she supposed to be the girl seen in the built-up haunted tower?" I asked.

"That I really can't say," she said. "There was a story often told in the old days that a beautiful embalmed girl in white lay in that tower, and it was there and near the castle that she used to appear to the people.[50] You know poor Castelar, the handsome minstrel, said and did some stupid things, and was beheaded[51] at the castle, and was probably buried near there. Get me from that shelf Whyte Melville's novel, 'The Queen's Maries.' "[52]

I did as she bade me.

---

[49] This is quite a humorous in-joke of Linskill's, as it was himself that had them installed when he was Dean of Guild for the town.

[50] This is a distortion by Linskill, attributing the White Lady to all sightings in this area. There are ghosts of three white ladies on the Scores path side of the Cathedral. Only one is the White Lady of the Haunted Tower. The others are Lady Buchan between the Castle and the entrance to Gregory Lane, and the White Lady of the Castle is Marion Ogilvy.

[51] As I mentioned in the previous footnote this was Pierre de Bocosel de Chastelard. He was hanged at the Mercat Cross in Market Square (now Market Street) in St Andrews on the 20th February 1563 for repeatedly hiding under the Queen's bed! That is fact. The suggestion of it being one of the lovely Mary Stuart's Maries is complete fiction.

[52] The book was a work of fiction published in 1862 by Major George John Whyte Melville, a novelist, poet and a golfing friend of Linskill's.

"Well, you will see there that the night before Castelar was to be beheaded kind Queen Mary sent one of her Maries, the one who loved Castelar, at her own special request to the castle with her ring to offer him a pardon if he left this country for ever.[53] This Marie did see Castelar, showed him the Queen's ring, and pleaded with him to comply, but he refused - he preferred death to banishment from his beloved Queen's Court, and the fair messenger left him obstinate in his dungeon.

This faithful Marie paced up and down all that night before the castle; then at dawn came the sound of a gun or culverin, a wreath of smoke floated out to sea, and Castelar was gone. Whyte Melville says she did not start, she did not shriek, nor faint, nor quiver, but she threw her hood back and looked wildly upward, gasping for air. Then as the rising sun shone on her bare head, Marie's raven hair was all streaked and patched with grey. When Mary Stuart fled to England, this faithful Marie, now no more needed, became a nun in St Andrews.

Look at page 371 of Whyte Melville's book," she said. So I read – "It was an early harvest that year in Scotland, but e'er the barley was white, Marie had done with nuns and nunneries, vows and ceremonies, withered hopes and mortal sorrows, and had gone to that place where the weary heart can alone find the rest it had so longed for at last."

The pathetic and the comic often go together. Just at this interesting point a cat sprang suddenly up and upset a cup of tea in the lap of my genial hostess. This created a diversion. Old ladies are apt to wander, which is annoying. She got clean away from her subject for a bit. She asked me if I knew Captain Robert Marshall, who wrote plays and "The Haunted Major."

I said I knew Bob well, and that he was an old Madras College boy. [54]

She then wanted to know if I knew how to pronounce the name of Mr Travis's American putter, and if Mr Low or I had ever tried it. She also wanted to know if I knew anything of the new patent clock worked on gramophone principles which shouted the homes instead of striking them.

Having answered all these queries to her satisfaction, and taken another cup of senna — I mean tea — I got her back to the White Lady.

"Oh, yes, my dear," she said, "I saw her, I and some friends. *A lot of us* had been out at Kinkell Braes one afternoon and stayed there long past the time allowed us. It was almost dark, and we scuttled up the brae from the Harbour rather frightened. Just near the turret light we saw the lady gliding along the top of the old Abbey wall. She was robed in a grey white dress with a veil over her head. She had raven black hair, and a string of beads hanging from her waist. We all huddled together, with our eyes and mouths wide open, and watched the figure. 'It's a girl sleep-walking,' I murmured.

'It's a bride,' whispered another. 'Oh! she'll fall,' said a little boy, grasping my arm. But she did not. She went inside the parapet wall at the Haunted Tower and vanished completely.

---

[54] Like myself, Captain Robert Marshall did attend Madras and Linskill knew him. He was a Captain in the 71st Highland Light Infantry. A Scottish author and playwright. His story *The Haunted Major* was a ghostly golfing yarn he published in 1902. It features a game of golf played at St Magnus (St Andrews) where the prize is the hand in marriage to a woman. The hero of the story is one Major John Gore who is playing very badly until the ghost of the Scottish Prelate Cardinal Smeaton comes to his aid against Gore's opponent called Lindsay. This is an inference on St Andrews history. Smeaton is Beaton who was killed at the Castle by Lindsay. He is described by the ghost in the book as one of his most determined foes who bewitches Gore's clubs to win the game against his arch enemy.

'It's a ghost; it's the White Lady,' we all shrieked, and ran off trembling home. My sister also saw her on one of the turrets in the Abbey wall, where she was seen by several people. Some months after, as I was doing my hair before my looking-glass, the same face looked over my shoulder, and I fainted. I have always felt an eerie feeling about a looking-glass ever since, even now, old woman as I am. Her lovely face is one never, never to be forgotten, having once seen it, but your new fashioned lamps have altered everything."

"And what do you think about it now" I asked her.

"I have told you all I know. The Lady used to be seen oftenest between the castle and that old turret. Perhaps she came to look at the last resting-place of her much loved and wayward minstrel, Castelar. Maybe she came to revisit the favourite haunts of her beloved girl Queen - truly called the Queen of the Roses; but to my dying day I shall never forget that face, that lovely, pathetic face I saw years ago, and which may still be seen by some. What! must you really go now; won't you have another cup of tea? Very well, good bye."

As I wended my way Clubwards I could not but think of the strange tale I had just heard and of Castelar's sad end, and I could not help wondering if I should ever be favoured with a sight of this beautiful White Lady.[55]

[55] This whole story is a mix of Chastelard's infatuation with the Queen and who was executed because of it, and the fictitious ballad of Mary Hamilton and a woman who may have been a chamber maid and executed for sleeping with the Queens second husband Lord Darnley. All is mixed with inspiration from the fictitious story by Whyte Melville.

The Veiled Nun of St. Leonards

Curiously enough, although I have been in many old haunted castles and churches (at the exact correct hour, viz., midnight) in Scotland, England, Wales, and the Rhine country, yet I have never been able to either see or hear a ghost of any sort. The only experience of the kind I ever had was an accidental meeting with the far-famed "Spring-heeled Jack" in a dark lane at Helensburgh. It was many years ago, and as I was then very small and he was of immense proportions, the meeting was distinctly unpleasant for me.

Now, from legends we learn that St. Andrews is possessed of a prodigious number of supernatural appearances of different kinds, sizes, and shapes – most of them of an awe-inspiring and blood curdling type. In fact, so numerous are they – 80 in number they seem to be – that there is really no room for any modem aspirants who may want a quiet place to appear and turn people's hair white. It might be well to mention a few of them before telling the tale of "The Veiled Nun of St Leonards Church Avenue."

We will put aside ordinary banshees and things that can only be heard. Well, there is the celebrated Phantom Coach that Willie Carson told us of. It has been heard and seen by many. There is also a white lady that used to haunt the Abbey Road, the ghost of St Rule's Tower, the Haunted Tower ghost, the Blackfriars ghost, the wraith of Hackston of Rathillet, the spectre of the old castle, the Dancing Skeletons, the smothered Piper Lad, the Phantom Bloodhound, the Priory Ghost, and many, many more. The Nun of St Leonards is as curious and interesting as any of them, though a bit weird and gruesome. In the time of charming Mary Stuart, our white Queen, there lived in the old South Street a very lovely lady belonging to a very old Scottish family, and her beauty and wit brought many admirers to claim her hand, but with little or no success. She waved them all away. At last she became affianced to a fine and brave young fellow who came from the East Lothian country, and for some months all went merrily as a marriage bell, but at last clouds overspread the rosy horizon. She resolved that she would never become an earthly bride, but would take the veil and become a bride of Holy Church – a nun, in point of fact. When her lover heard that she had left home and entered a house of Holy Sisters, he at once announced his intention of hastening to St. Andrews, seizing her, and marrying her at once. In this project it would seem the young lady's parents were in perfect agreement with the devoted youth. He did hasten to St. Andrews almost immediately, and there received a terrible shock. On meeting this once lovely and loved maiden, he discovered that she had actually done what she had threatened to do. Sooner than be an earthly bride she had mutilated her face by slitting her nostrils and cutting off her eyelids and both her top and bottom lips, and had branded her fair cheeks with cruel hot irons.

The poor youth, on seeing her famous beauty thus destroyed, fled to Edinburgh, where he committed suicide, and she, after becoming a nun, died from grief and remorse. That all happened nearly 400 years ago; but her spirit with the terribly marred and mutilated face still wanders o' nights in the peaceful little avenue to old St Leonards iron kirk gate down the Pends Road. She is all dressed in black, with a long black veil over the once lovely face, and carries a lantern in her hand. Should any bold visitor in that avenue meet her, she slowly sweeps her face veil aside, raises the lantern to her scarred face, and discloses those awful features to his horrified gaze. Here is a curious thing that I know happened there a few years ago.

I knew a young fellow here who was reading up theology and Church canon law. I also knew a great friend of his, an old Cambridge man. The former I will call Wilson, and the latter Talbot, as I do not want to give the exact names. Well, Wilson had invited Talbot up to St. Andrews for a month of golf, and he arrived here on a Christmas day. He came to my rooms for about ten minutes, and I never saw anyone merrier and brighter and full of old days at Cambridge. Then he hurried off to see the Links and the Club. Late that evening Wilson rushed in. "Come along quick and see Talbot; he's awfully ill, and I don't know what's up a bit." I went off and found Talbot in his lodgings with a doctor in attendance, and he certainly looked dangerously ill, and seemed perfectly dazed. Wilson told me that he had to go to see some people on business that evening down by the harbour, and that he took Talbot with him down the Pends Road. It was a fine night, and Talbot said he would walk about the road and enjoy a cigar till his friend's return. In about half-an-hour Wilson returned up the Pends Road, but could see Talbot nowhere in sight. After hunting about for a long time, he found him leaning against the third or fourth tree up the little avenue to St Leonards kirk gate.

He went up to him, when Talbot turned a horrified face towards him, saying, "Oh, my God, have you come to me again?" and fell down in a fit or a swoon. He got some passers-by to help to take poor Talbot to his rooms. Then he came round to me. We sat up with him in wonder and amazement; and, briefly, this is what he told us. After walking up and down the Pends Road, he thought he would take a survey of the little avenue, when at the end he saw a light approaching him, and turned back to meet it. Thinking it was a policeman, he wished him "Good evening," but got no reply. On approaching nearer he saw it to be a veiled female with a lantern. Getting quite close, she stopped in front of him, drew aside her long veil, and held up the lantern towards him. "My God," said Talbot, "I can never forget or describe that terrible, fearful face. I felt choked, and I fell like a log at her feet. I remember no more till I found myself in these rooms, and you two fellows sitting beside me. I leave this place tomorrow" – and he did by the first train. His state of panic was terrible to see. Neither Wilson nor Talbot had ever heard the tale of the awful apparition of the St Leonards nun, and I had almost forgotten the existence of the strange story till so curiously reminded of it. I never saw Talbot again, but I had a letter from him a year after written from Rhienfells, telling me that on Christmas day he had had another vision, dream, or whatever it was, of the same awful spectre. About a year later I read in a paper that poor old Talbot had died on Christmas night at Rosario of heart failure. I often wonder if the dear old chap had had another visit from the terrible Veiled Nun of St Leonards Avenue.

Note from Richard

Regarding the number of ghosts in St Andrews, Linskill mentions '80 in number they seem to be'. I mentioned in my introduction there are currently over 300 individual ghosts in St Andrews, had Linskill been aware of this, like most, he would have been astounded at the number, and far from trying to find a quiet space to turn people's hair white, we have a bit of a ghost fest going on in St Andrews. Not all are historic, far from it but all are current. It is not just the nun who watches you when you are in the avenue. There is another ghost. Her name is Bella. She started appearing on tours in November 2018. I have a fair number of mediums on my tours and they are the ones who have spoken to me about her. It was a couple from Glasgow who first mentioned her. I then kept her quiet to see if any others would pick her up. They did, on 12 independent occasions - all before anyone else was aware of her.

There has also been mild poltergeist activity that we have all experienced on different tours occurring between 2018 and 2020. Bella stands opposite the nun in the avenue and comes on some of my tours. I caught a glimpse of her in November 2020. We all heard a shuffling noise, when I looked, there she was, the light shadow of a girl, standing between the tree and the wall in the avenue. By the time the others turned she had disappeared behind the tree. It was the fact there was no one there that scared them.

The Veiled Nun of St. Leonards

The nun is the only ghost Linskill gives mention to out of 31 attested ghosts either in the buildings or grounds of St Leonards. When this was the priory precincts there was a nunnery here which makes sense of her being seen in this vicinity. Set in the Nun's Walk, Linskill in his story gives its actual title, 'St Leonards Church Avenue,' the name 'Nun's Walk' developed as a consequence of his story. So much so, unless they can remember reading his story few are aware of what its actual name is. There is a plaque on the southern wall to the walk that even records it as being the Nun's Walk and gives mention to the ghost, but this is a reference to Linskill's ghost, not to the reality of what people have witnessed, so it shows the impact his story has had.

The majority of those experiencing the ghosts of St Andrews have never heard of Linskill or his stories, but they have experienced the monk of St Rules, the White Lady, the phantom coach and the nun amongst many others. The nun has been seen in the garden of Queen Mary's House, standing opposite St Leonards Chapel, seated within the Chapel, standing at the altar, and walking through the south entrance to the chapel. In recent years she has also been seen standing by the tree next to the Half Moon gates in the Nun's Walk in 2012, 2013, 2016 and 2018. She has never been seen anywhere else in St Andrews apart from these locations. Barring the garden ghost, it is the same person in the five other locations. Other than being a nun I do not know who she is, or why she is still here, but I do know this is her spirit. She is aware of those who step into her sphere of involvement, she is shy and she will watch you.

For the most part, a ghost will appear as real as you and I. It is only when they defy the laws of physics, or something about them is out of place or out of sync that we are alerted to their otherworldly nature. A commonality is to think it is someone in fancy dress or in costume, then feeling something isn't right they become unnerved when the penny drops for what they are observing – if they do at all at the time. More often, it is not until later when the true nature of these experience becomes apparent. It tends to start with an unaccountable niggling feeling, turning into the realisation that whatever occurred was physically impossible. The impression of the moment is something that never leaves you.

These are traits in-keeping with most observances or encounters as the mind tries to work out the logic of what it sees. The following is again in-keeping with this:

When I saw the nun back in July 2017 with 10 students at St Leonards, she was silhouetted against a bright halogen light opposite the chapel. We observed her as we walked towards her, and when we reached about halfway to the school grounds she moved behind a tree. Everyone saw her and comments in a joking manner were made that, "a school pupil is going to jump out at us when we get to the tree," but when we arrived, no one was there. In a bid to work out the logic of what we had just observed for a good minute, they were looking down for a trapdoor, and up to see if she had climbed the tree. That is when they got spooked.

We all saw her as a silhouette, so when I ask those who have seen her closeup if she had a veil, and if her face was mutilated, they look at me somewhat confused as to why I had just asked them those questions, and each time with a shake of their head their reply is to the negative. So, let it be known, the nun is very real, the veil, the mutilated face is Linskill's fiction. There is no lantern and there is certainly no backstory, that is all Linskill's fiction, including the tale about Talbot seeing her and becoming unhinged.

On gathering a particular pace and popularity over the years, it is Linskill's backstories that have ensnared the imagination of many, then through the grapevine, they have been picked up by authors, editors or publishers, adding a spice they know will have more impact. Peter Underwood's brief accounts of a few St Andrews ghosts in his book *Gazetteer of Scottish Ghosts* in 1973, is a good example of this.

So where did Linskill get the inspiration for his story?

It was certainly based on the apparition of the nun in the avenue, which in his day was a very picturesque tree lined avenue. The basis for his story and the involvement of the nun he gained from Whyte Melville's fictional story *The Bride of Heaven*. In Linskill's story - '*Concerning More Appearances of the White Lady*', one of the Four Maries becomes a nun. Then following from that an elderly woman speaking with Linskill says, ' "Look at page 371 of Whyte Melville's book." So I read – "It was an early harvest that year in Scotland, but e'er the barley was white, Marie had done with nuns and nunneries, vows and ceremonies, withered hopes and mortal sorrows, and had gone to that place where the weary heart can alone find the rest it had so longed for at last." '

That is a direct quote from Melville.

Linskill builds this into his story of the White Lady, intimating that having been a nun she had then died. Melville in his book however continues (which Linskill doesn't)… "tomorrow she would become the Bride of Heaven, and *the veil she would then put on must never be taken off again this side of the grave!*' This is crucial to Linskill's Veiled Nun tale. "*Never taken off this side of the grave*".

So he borrowed the veil from Melville, reinforced by reports of the shrouded White Lady in the Cathedral grounds. The location was easy, as there was already the ghost of a nun there, so what about the mutilated features?

Of the vast amount of reports I have published, I have included the following from 1988 as it gives his source. During my early researches, Jane Kilpatrick, a fourth year of the University in 1988, approached me with her experience whilst walking back to her residence at the Gatty a few evenings before. Once past the Haunted Tower she saw a woman standing on the grass in front of her. She was standing quite still and silent between a bench and the high Cathedral Wall. Her arms were stretched out as if leaning on the back of a bench. Drawing closer the woman was quite tall, young, slim, with long dark hair and wearing a long pale green dress, quite plain in design with sleeves puffing out at the wrists. Around her waist hung what she thought to be a belt, the same colour as the dress and tied at the middle. As she drew closer a strange feeling crept over her, an impression that the figure did not belong in our own time at all – which is very common. It was a very eerie feeling she couldn't quite explain.

The woman seemed solid enough at first, but when about ten feet away, she seemed to fade as if merging a little with the wall behind, but not becoming transparent. It was dark by this time but the moon was shining clearly and the street lamps lighting the way were enough for her to see by.

The figure was gazing at her with "a fixed intensity," as she put it, almost menacingly, which coupled with a looming fear made her feel cold and uneasy. No actual expression was to be found from the woman, but the right side of her face had been badly disfigured, distorting her eye. This startled her. It didn't appear to be a natural disfigurement but something having occurred whilst alive.

She carried on walking, and made no attempt to communicate with this figure but found it hard to take her gaze off whatever it was she was seeing. On passing this curious woman, she then became aware of it seeming to follow her. The Cathedral Wall at this point on the Kirkheugh veers away more to the right at an angle to the pathway. Rather than follow her on the path, the woman followed pace but kept on the grass by the course of the Cathedral Wall. On reaching the steps leading down to the harbour by the old Kirk ruins she noticed the apparition out the corner of her eye and turned to look. The 'Green Lady' as it were, was now standing by the wall some thirty feet away from where she was. Her hands were clasped in front of her and still staring as menacingly as before. Feeling very unnerved Jane ran the rest of the way to her residences.

Upon arrival, she was quite out of breath, and by all accounts was looking very pale. Her friends gave her a cup of tea and held a certain amount of disbelief to start with when she relayed her experience to them, but whatever they made of her account, they had no doubt at all that whatever it was she saw that evening had frightened her, and disturbed her greatly. When I interviewed her, she was still visibly shaken as the moment was very fresh in her mind.

The realisation of what you have always been led to believe was fiction comes at a price - it does change your life. As a note; the Old Harbour Road followed the precinct wall more closely than the path does now and slopped down directly from the Lighthouse Turret to the Harbour like a ravine (hence Kirkheugh, a heugh is a ravine), but there may have been an embankment from the road to the wall.

Add the disfigured apparition of Kirkheugh to Linskill's tale, the veil of Melville's Marie and her reaction to the death of Castelar... "she threw her hood back and looked wildly..." Then throw in a lantern to highlight the mutilated features to give it a more nocturnal drama; superimpose it all on an existing ghost of the nun in St Leonards Chapel Avenue, and you now know how the most famous ghost story in St Andrews was born!

As a point of interest, on reading a little further down the page in Melville's book we find his fictitious Marie (his White Lady) never actually became a nun in St Andrews after all that. He says, "There is little doubt she would have fulfilled her intention had the occasion ever arrived." In Melville's story the occasion never arose because she died before she had a chance, which is why he says "Marie had done with nuns and nunneries... and had gone to that place where the weary heart can alone find the rest it had so longed for at last." Linskill had switched round Melville's story!

George John Whyte Melville
1821-1878[56]

This is the Melville of Mount Melville Estate, you may know part of it as being Craigtoun. He also owned neighbouring Bogward Estate. Perhaps you are familiar with the fountain in Market Street and never paid much attention to it other than it is never being used as a fountain? This is a memorial fountain built in Melville's honour in 1880, and made of Dumfries sandstone, the same as Hamilton Grand. It was only operational a few times due to a shortage of fresh water. In 2014, the council spent a lot of money attending to this fountain to make it operational again. Only to find health and safety objected to its being turned on in case a gust of wind blew the spouting water onto a windscreen and caused an accident. One must wonder what Rome would make of Fife's health and safety's cautionary ingenuity. Being a city of over 2000 fountains and many roundabouts, what do you suppose the traffic circumnavigates as these roundabouts? giant 2000-year-old spectacularly carved white marble fountains, and all fully functioning in graceful perpetuity!

I am sure the next time you look at Melville's fountain, no little irony will spring to mind, but think also on Linskill's inspiration for the most famous ghost story in St Andrews.

But I digress, let's see what Linskill's next ghoulish yarn holds in store for us.

---

[56] From the National Portrait Gallery, London

A Spiritualistic Seance

THE M'Whiskers, whom I met at Oban, were very jolly old people. Papa M'Whisker had made a big fortune teaplanting in Ceylon, and had bought, and added to Dramdotty Castle in the far, far north. They were perfectly full of ghosts and spiritualism, and at Dramdotty they seemed to have a ghost for every day in the week. On Monday there was the "Spotted Nun," on Tuesday the "Floating Infant," on Wednesday the "Headless Dwarf," on Thursday the "Vanishing Negro," on Friday the "Burnt Lady," and on Saturday the "Human Balloon," and on Sunday the whole lot attended on them, and, I daresay, went to the kirk with them.

M'Whisker himself was a jovial soul, fond of his toddy, and very much resembled the Dougal Cratur in "Rob Roy." My friend, John Clyde, should have seen him. He had a furious red head of hair and beard of the same colour, and the street boys used to call after him the song, "The folks all call me Carroty, What, what, what, oh! Carroty," etc. Mrs M'Whisker was a stout lady with eyes like small tomatoes and a gimlet nose. They had a son, a boy of ten, called Fernando M'Whisker, because he was born in Spain. When they came to St. Andrews they had purchased a number of my "Ghost Books." (These ghosts at present chiefly haunt the *Citizen* Warehouse, booksellers' shops, and the railway bookstall.) That is the reason perhaps that the M'Whiskers invited me to a spiritualistic seance at their house in South Street. They generally came to St. Andrews for the winter, partly to get away from the cold of their northern home, and partly because they thought the history and atmosphere of St. Andrews lent itself to an all-pervading presence of ghosts, spooks, and spirits. I had only been to two such shows before - one at Helensburgh and one at Cambridge - and was, and still am, very doubtful of the genuineness of spiritualism.[57] On the day appointed I went to the M'Whiskers' house in South Street, and was shown in by a Highlander in the M'Whisker tartan. It was early in the afternoon, but I found the shutters in the large room all shut, and a few dim lights only were burning. On a sideboard in the corner stood plenty of refreshments and everything else to comfort the inner man. In the centre of the room there was a round table covered with a M'Whisker tartan tablecloth, which touched the floor all round: this in itself was suspicious to my mind. I was introduced to the chief medium, one Mr Peter Fancourt, who looked as if he had been buried and dug up again. He was in tight, sleek black clothes, and resembled in every way "Uriah Heep" in "David Copperfield." The other medium was a Mrs Flyflap Corncockle. They were supposed not to know each other, but I am as certain that they were accomplices as that the Bell Rock is near St. Andrews Bay. A number of chairs encircled the table. We had all to seat ourselves on these chairs, with our thumbs and little fingers touching round the edge of the table. The first thing that happened was a kind of "squish," and then a huge bouquet of flowers descended on the table from somewhere. It was a clever trick, but the flowers were of the commonest sort, and what I had seen in all the greengrocers' shops that morning. The lights were now turned very low, and a spirit arm and hand appeared floating about, which shone a good deal. It hovered about from the ceiling to above our heads, and when I got a chance I jumped on a chair and seized it with both hands. It seemed to shrink up, and was torn through my

---

[57] As I mentioned in the introduction it was to the fraudulent mediums he had a distain for, which is what we have here. His scepticism for spiritualism and even ghosts is a front for his stories. Taking on the role of devil's advocate with an almost Jekyll and Hyde approach. He presents this dichotomy as hooks to promote through surprise or to decry through cynicism what he hears. As I also mentioned, his stories are a minefield of fiction, half-truths and truths. As you may have gathered, if Linskill says something is true - it isn't, he is playing on emphasis to draw you in.

hands very forcibly, and in such a material manner that I was forced to let go. I don't know where the hand and arm went to, but it was simply a juggling trick. After this "Mr Heep" (I beg his pardon, Mr Fancourt) said that there was an unbeliever present, and as I was that unbeliever I was relegated to an armchair by the fireplace with one of M'Whisker's muckle cigars. From that point of vantage I watched the whole affair, and they assured me they would tell me all that was going on. The next very curious thing was that they suddenly all took their hands off the table, and their eyes slowly followed something ceilingwards. It was funny to see them all lying back staring up at the roof. Then very slowly their heads and eyes resumed their normal position.

"Did you see that?" said the M'Whisker triumphantly. "I saw nothing whatever," I remarked. "What! did you not see the table float up to the ceiling? It remained there quite half a second, and then came down as lightly as a feather." "I was watching the table the whole time," I said, "and it never moved an inch from its place."

"Oh! you are an unbeliever," said Mrs M'Whisker sadly, "but later on when it is darker you will see Mr Fancourt float out of one of the windows and come in at the other." I fervently hoped if he did anything of the kind he would come a cropper on the pavement below and break some of his ribs. The table then started to dance about and move along, but this, I am certain, was simply engineered by those two mediums.

After some tomfoolery of this kind they all agreed that "Ouija" should be brought out. A large oblong yellow board was then produced and laid on the table. On it were the letters of the alphabet and a number of figures, also the sun, moon, and stars, and some other fantastic symbols. On this board was placed a small table with a round body and round head, it had three hind legs and a front, which was the pointer. These legs had little red velvet boots on. The two mediums then placed their hands on each side of this curious table, which immediately began to run about to the letters and figures, spelling out things and fixing dates in answer to questions asked. It was not the least like a planchette, which is on wheels. The first thing they informed me it had said was that a spirit called Clarissa was present, and for many years she had lain dying in that room. She maintained that she was some distant relation of the White Lady of the Haunted Tower. It then rushed into poetry. Its first effort was the "Legend of Purple James and his Girl," a comic thing which reminded me of the "Bab Ballads."[58] They afterwards gave me a copy of this poem, which I still possess. Next the spirit gave us a Scotch poem about a haggis, and then one called "Edward and the Hard-Boiled Egg." It then devoted its attention to me, whom it characterised as the "Unbeliever." It stated that if the Antiquarian Society would dig a pit four feet square by six feet deep between the two dungeons in the Kitchen Tower of the castle, and if the rock were cut through, a cave would be found full of casks of good red wine. On no condition whatever would I, on such evidence, recommend the Society to strike a pick in there. The next spirit that turned up was one Jaspar Codlever. He alluded to me as "the Cambridge man in the chair with the cigar." He said that if excavations were made between the two last trees in Lawpark Wood a stone cist would be found full of Pictish ornaments.[59] Again he told us that within a cave on the cliffs there was a chalice of great value placed there by Isabella the Nun, who still guarded it by night and day, and was very dangerous to approach. This spirit then went away, and his place was taken by a monk named Rudolph, who informed us that the entrance to the Crypt or sub-Chapel was between

[58] Bab was the pen name of W. S. Gilbert of Gilbert and Sullivan fame, and the ballads are a collection of poems or light verse.
[59] Law Park Wood is situated at the end of the Lade Braes by an ancient Mill Pond, which is by Hallow Hill; the site of a Celtic long cist cemetery where over 140 graves were uncovered by archaeologists 1975-77. The site was first discovered in 1867, and was the sister community to that of Kirkheugh by the harbour from the sixth to ninth century.

two of the pillars in the Priory. As there are a lot of pillars there, it is impossible to know which he meant.[60] He said this entrance was near Roger's tomb. Who Roger may be I know not.[61] He then told us about this Crypt. He said there was something so horrible in it that it turned him sick. Curiously enough, some thought-reading people told us the same story in the Town Hall some years ago, but they said the underground Chapel was at the east end of the Cathedral. The monk then went on to tell us of this place in the Priory. He said it had Purbeck marble pillars, a well of clear water, and three small costly altars, and a number of books of the Vincentian Canons. There was a short interval now, and the lights were turned up. I was anxious to get away, but they implored me to stay and see the cabinet and the spirits therein. I told them in my most dramatic fashion that I was late already, and I had a meeting on. M'Whisker then begged me, if I would not stay to see the spirits, to taste some, and he mixed me an excellent whisky-and-soda, which he called a "Blairgowrie." I then made my adieu, and was very glad to get once more into the street and also into a world of sense. The M'Whiskers informed me some days afterwards that they were very sorry at my leaving, as, after I had gone, Fancourt had floated out of the window, and numerous wonderful spirits had appeared in the cabinet. I am glad I went when I did, as I should certainly have taken a poker to that cabinet.

---

[60] The logical place would be between the last and second last pillars of the South Transept by the old Priory, on the far right when looking from the direction of the Cathedral entrance. It is where myself and others saw the White Lady on two occasions.

[61] Bishop Roger De Beaumont was Bishop of St Andrews from 1189. Dying in 1202, he was buried in the Cathedral grounds. Building of the new Cathedral had begun in 1160 to replace St. Regulus Cathedral. Bishop Roger continued overseeing its construction and also built the Castle as an Episcopal Palace shortly before his death.

The Apparition of
Sir Roger de Wanklin[62]

I AM very fond indeed of Christmas time. There has been little snow this season. I think it has forgotten how to snow in these days. Still, I always feel Christmassy. I think of the good old coaching days, when there was really snow, of Washington, Irving, and good old Dickens and Scott, of the yule log and the family gatherings and reunions, of the wassail bowl, of frumenty and plum porridge, and mince pies, plum puddings, and holly and mistletoe and big dances in the servants' hall, of good old ancestral ghosts and hearty good cheer.

I am sitting to-day in a cosy armchair (of the old school, no modern fake) talking to my old friend, Theophilus Greenbracket. Filus, as I call him, is a clever man of many parts; he is a great traveller and sportsman, and takes a deep interest in every mortal thing. There is nothing of the kill joy or fossil about Greenbracket; he is up-to-date and true blue.

He is sitting opposite me smoking a gigantic cigar and imbibing rum punch, and talking hard; he always talks hard, but is never a bore, and never palls on one in the slightest degree. He has an enormous dog at his feet, with a fierce, vindictive expression, which belies its real nature, as it is gentle with everything and everybody, except cats and rats. Greenbracket is, among many other things, a great spiritualist and visionary, and possesses all kinds of mediumistic appliances, such as pythos, planchettes and ouijas, which he works with his old butler, Amos Bradleigh, who is another spirit hunter.

---

[62] Sir Roger de Wanklin was Sir James Hamilton of Finnart, (c.1495–1540). This is Linskill's Catholic humour, as he was known as the bastard of Arran. The illegitimate half-brother of the Earl of Arran and noted architect to King James V. He was involved in the construction of Stirling Castle Falkland Palace, the original part of Holyrood Palace and the Royal residence of the New Inn at St Andrews.

"By the bye," said Greenbracket, "I am at present taking lessons in music with Mr Easeboy." He says this so suddenly that he makes me jump, as we were talking about sea serpents and the probability of their existence.

"Are you indeed, old chap," I said.

"Yes, thorough bass, and consecutive fifths and harmony and all that sort of thing, you know. He has a pupil, Macbeth Churchtimber, who has just written a thundering pretty waltz called "Eleanor Wynne.""

"I thought Churchtimber," I mildly suggested, "only played severe classical stuff."

"Oh, yes," replied my friend, "but he occasionally touches on a lighter theme, and has even written a comic song, called, 'I lay beside a milestone with a sunflower on my brow.'"

"I must try it someday," I said, "but how about your ghosts? Have you seen any lately?"

"There was one here a few minutes ago," said Greenbracket, "a tall man in armour sitting in that corner over there."

"What rubbish," I said, quite crossly, "you dream things, or drink, or eat too much."

"No I don't," said Greenbracket, "do you really mean to tell that you felt no sensation just now, no pricking or tingling feeling, or a chilly sensation down your back?"

"Certainly not, nothing of the kind," I replied.

"Well, that is queer," he said, "I know you don't see these things, but I fancied you would have felt a strange presence in some way. I don't know who the man in armour was. I have not seen him before, but my butler has, at all events. It was not Sir Roger de Wanklyn."

'Who the ------ is he?" I queried.

"Oh," said my host, "he is the earth-bound spirit of an architect who lived in St. Andrews at the time that James the Fifth married Mary of Lorraine in the Cathedral; he says he was present at the ceremony and can describe it all. A gay pageant it was and much revelry." [63]

"If you can get all this sort of curious information, which I don't exactly credit, why on earth can't you find out something practical and useful, for instance, where the secret underground hiding place is, and where all the tons of valuable ornaments, papers, and vestments are concealed?"

"My dear friend," said Greenbracket solemnly, "these people won't be pumped; they only tell you what they choose to, or are permitted to reveal."

"If they really do turn up and talk to you as you say they do, why on earth can't you get them to talk some useful sense?"

"I really can't force their confidence," said Greenbracket, "all they do tell me voluntarily is most interesting and absorbing. This Sir Rodger planned numerous very important structural alterations in the Cathedral and elsewhere."

"It is all very odd to me," I said, "one meets people with strange ideas. I met a man years ago at Aberystwyth who was a firm believer in the transmigration of souls. He said he quite remembered being a cab horse in Glasgow, and was certain when he left this planet he would become a parrot in Mars."

"I don't understand that sort of thing a bit," said my extraordinary friend, Greenbracket, "but Sir Rodger de Wanklyn has sometimes to visit the Valley of Fire and Frost, where there are mighty furnaces on one side of him and ice and snow on the other and it is very painful."

"I had that sort of experience the other day," I remarked, "at a meeting. On one side was a furnace of fire, on the other a window wide open with a biting frost wind blowing in."

---

[63] The wedding in France was by Proxy on 9th May 1538 as James V was still in Scotland, the 'marriage' in St Andrews was a confirmation by both in person on June 18th 1538, following the arrival of Mary and her retinue. It was possible to have both a proxy wedding followed by a marriage ceremony where both parties were present, but strictly speaking the sacrament was in France.

"Tuts," said Greenbracket "that's here; I am talking of the spirit world."

"Hang! your spirit stuff. Has your butler, Amos Bradleigh, seen any spooky things lately?"

"Yes, he is much annoyed by the spirit of an evil old housekeeper here who lost her life by falling downstairs, and she is continually pushing him down my cellar stairs. He is furious."

"Is this butler of yours any connection of Jeremiah Anklebone?" I asked.

"Yes, he is a cousin," said Greenbracket; "all that family have second sight, and see and dream strange things."

"And who," I asked, "may this housekeeper be who pitched your butler down stairs?"

"Oh," said Greenbracket, "she's a badly constituted wraith, and her name is Annibal Strongthorn. She was housekeeper ages ago to this Sir Roger de Wanklyn in this very old house we are in."

"What happened to this Sir Roger? Has he told you?"

"Oh! yes he fell over the cliffs."

"Bless me, and did this old housekeeper woman push him over. Was she a murderess?"

"Oh, how can I tell," said Greenbracket peevishly, "he has told me nothing of the kind."

"Well, old fellow," I said, "you really do not get much interesting information out of your ghostly friends, but what I like about you is that all your numerous ghosts come straight to you, straight to head-quarters at once – you don't go fooling about with chairs and tables and sideboards and other pieces of timber in an idiotic way. If, as some people say, they can get chairs and tables and other articles of furniture to follow them about, why don't they go in for cheap furniture removals at night when the streets are empty?"

"Don't make a joke of everything," said Greenbracket, "I do see and converse with departed spirits. I do not ask them to come; they come to me, and half of them I have never heard of before or thought of either."

"May I ask, my good friend Greenbracket, what sort of clothes they wear when they pay you these visits; for instance, what does your latest apparition. Sir Rodger, clothe himself in?"

"Bless me!" said Theophilus, "why in the dress of his times, of course – a jerken, doublet, and hose, a rapier, and all that sort of thing; sometimes he wears a sort of coarse fustian cassock with a double breast."

"I can't make out," I said to my spiritualistic friend, "where these clothes come from. Have they got a sort of theatrical wardrobe wherever they are existing? If so, why can't the ghosts of old world clothes come alone? In such a case you might see a modern suit of evening togs, or armour, or boots and spurs, or military dress walk into your room without anything inside them; or you might, with a stretch of imagination, see a suit of pyjamas, or a pair of slippers going about the place."

"Shut up talking like that," said Theophilus, "you don't possess the sense – I mean the extra sense to see these beings; but read this document I have written out. Surely it will convince you that I really do get valuable inspirations from other worlds, but, mind, keep it a strict secret at present."

"All right, I promise you," I murmured placidly. Then I perused carefully the more than extraordinary document he had handed me.

"It is very curious," I said, "if it be one bit true; and if genuine, might be extremely useful. Mind my lips are sealed. But from whom did you obtain this remarkable story?"

"From Sir Rodger de Wanklyn, the Cathedral architect," he replied, and off I went quite full of my queer friend. Greenbracket, and of Annabel Strongthorn, Amos Bradleigh, and his cousin Anklebone, and particularly Rodger de Wanklyn.

The Bewitched Ermentrude

Very many years ago now I was sauntering down historic old South Street one November afternoon, my object being to lunch in one of the quaint houses with my old time friend, Harold Slitherwick. Lunch was not, however, the main object of my visit, but to meet a man called Reginald Saedegar, an ex-Indian judge, who had actually seen a genuine spirit or ghost.

It is a sad, nay, a melancholy fact (for I have been told this by the very best authorities) that *I am not Psychic*, despite the fact that I have spent days and nights in gloomy, grimly-haunted chambers and ruins, and even a lonesome Halloween night on the summit of St Rule's ancient Tower (my only companions being sandwiches, matches, some cigars, and the necessary and indispensable flask[64]), yet, alas! I have *never* heard or seen anything the least abnormal, or felt the necessary, or much-talked-of mystic presence.[65]

Arriving at the old mansion, I was duly ushered in by Slitherwick's butler, one Joe Bingworthy, a man with the manner and appearance of an archbishop, and from whom one always seemed to expect a sort of pontifical blessing.

There were several fellows there, and I was speedily made known to Saedeger, a very cheery, pleasant little person, with dark hair and big eyebrows.

There was a very heated discussion going on when I entered as to what was really a properly constituted Cathedral. Darkwood was shouting, "No Bishop's Chair, *no* Cathedral." "If," he said, "a Bishop had his chair in a tiny chapel, it was a Cathedral, but if a religious building was as big as the Crystal Palace, and there was no Bishop's Chair there, it was not one bit a Cathedral."

---

[64] Brandy
[65] As you know he did!

I stopped this discussion suddenly by asking Saedegar about his ghost, and was told I would hear the whole story after lunch.

Before we adjourned to the smoke room Saedeger was telling us he felt a bit knocked up with his long journey. He had a thirty-six hours' journey after he left good old Tony-Pandy. Visions of "Tony Lumpkin," and "Tony Faust," in "My Sweetheart," flitted through my brain, then I suddenly remembered, luckily, that "Tony-pandy" was a town in Wales.

Once comfortably seated in the smoke-room with pipes, cigars, and whisky, Reginald Saedeger became at once the centre of all the interest.

"Lots of years ago," he said, in a quiet legal voice, "I came to visit some friends in St. Andrews, and I had a most unaccountable experience. I will tell you all about it. I never saw anything supernatural before, and have never seen anything the least remarkable since; but one night, my first night in that house, I undoubtedly saw the wraith of the 'Blue Girl.'"

"What had you for supper that evening?" I mildly asked.

"Only chicken and salad," was the reply. "I was not thinking of anything ghostly. If you fix your mind *intently* on one thing, as some folk can, you can self-hypnotise yourself. I had no idea but golf in my mind when I went off to roost."

"Well, drive ahead," said I.

"I had a charming, comfortable, big old-world room given me, nice fire, and all that sort of thing," continued Saedeger, "and as I was deuced tired I soon went to bed and to sleep.

"I woke suddenly, later, with the firm conviction that a pair of eyes were fixed on me. I suppose everyone knows that if you stare fixedly at any sleeping person, they will soon awake. I got a start when I half-opened my eyes, for leaning on the mantelpiece staring hard at me in the mirror was a most beautiful girl in a light blue gauzy dress, her back, of course, was to the bed, and I saw she had masses of wavy, golden-brown hair hanging down long past her waist.

"I was utterly astonished, and watched the movements of this beautiful creature with my eyes almost closed. I felt sure it was someone in the house having a lark at my expense, so pretended to be asleep. As I watched, the girl turned round and faced me, and I marvelled at the extraordinary loveliness of her figure and features. I wondered if she was a guest in the house, and what she was doing wandering about at that time of night, and if she was sleep-walking? She then glided – it certainly *was not walking* – to a corner of the room, and then I noticed that her feet were bare. She seemed to move along above the carpet – not on it – a curious motion. She drifted, and stood beneath a big picture, took out a key and opened a small aumbrey, or cupboard, in the wall quite noiselessly. And from this receptacle she took out some small things that glittered in her pretty fingers, long taper fingers."

"How on earth did you contrive to see all that in a dark bedroom?" I sarcastically inquired.

"The room wasn't dark," said Saedeger. "I always keep the light burning in a strange house and in a strange room."

"Oh, I see," I replied. "Go on."

"Well," continued Reginald Saedeger, "she then turned and came towards the bed, and I got a more distinct view of her. I had never seen anyone a bit like her before; it was an utterly unforgettable face. I have certainly never before, or since, seen anyone as pretty as she was – yet it was a strange, unearthly beauty, and her huge forget-me-not blue eyes were a perfection of pathos. Nearer, and yet nearer, she came, and when quite close to the bed, she bent over me and raised her hand with the glittering thing in it high over my head. Then I made a tremendous spring out of bed, crying loudly, 'Now I'll see who is trying to frighten me.' I flung out my arms to grasp her, but they closed on nothing, and to my utter astonishment I saw her standing smiling at me on the opposite side of the room.

"That was odd and uncanny enough, but then she gradually began to disappear, dissolving into a thin blue-grey mist, until nothing whatever remained – I was absolutely alone in the room and dumfounded"

"What next?" I asked.

"Well! what could I do or think?" said Saedeger. "I was fairly flabbergasted at the unexpected turn of events. I admit I felt shaky, so I took a stiff whisky and soda, smoked a pipe, and went back to bed to reflect on the matter, and fell asleep. I was wakened in the morning by my host, Harold Slitherwick, walking into the room carrying a pony brandy for me."

"Well, old blighter, how have you slept?" he asked.

"Then I told him about the blue girl."

"Bless my heart! Have you seen her too? Lots of people, my wife among the number, declare they have seen her; but as you have seen her now, I really begin to believe there is some truth in the tale."

"I then told my host there was no dubiety about the matter, and pointed out the place under the picture where there was a cupboard. We both went and looked. There was no cupboard to be seen."

"Very rum thing," said my host; "there was a murder once took place in this room ages ago. Perhaps the blue lady had something to do with it; but let us hunt for your cup- board."

"On rapping with our knuckles on the wall we found a hollow spot, scraped off the paper, and there sure enough was the little door I had seen. We soon forced it open, and discovered a receptacle, about a foot square, going very deep into the thick stone wall. There were a lot of things in that place, scissors, a thimble, a dagger, a work-box, and a lot of old musty, dusty papers. And then we found a long tress of ruddy-gold hair in an envelope and a beautiful miniature magnificently painted on ivory of the blue girl I had seen – every detail, the face, the dress, the hair, and the bare feet, were perfectly exact. On both the envelope and the miniature were written the names 'Ermentrude Ermengarde Annibal Beaurepaire,' with the date 1559.

"We then examined the old documents which gave us some clue to the mystery. It was a very long story that we had to read over, but I will tell it to you briefly. Long ages ago this ancient house was the property of a Frenchman, Monsieur Louis Beaurepaire. He had an only and lovely daughter of twenty, named Ermentrude Ermengarde Annibal Beaurepaire, who was intended to be a bride of the Church, otherwise a nun. This idea, apparently, did not appeal to her views. She passionately loved a young student, and was equally beloved by him, whose name was Eugene Malvoisine.

"All went well it seems, for two years, and they were to be married in the Cathedral at Easter. All the arrangements were complete for the nuptials; but fortune is a fickle jade, and willed it otherwise. A rival turned up on the scene in the person of Marie de Mailross, a cousin of the Beaurepaires, and a frequent guest at their house. Ermentrude found that her beloved Eugene had proved faithless, and transferred his youthful affections to the lovely Marie, and that a speedy elopement was pending.

"Ermentrude went and consulted a wise woman, otherwise a witch, who resided in Argyll, outwith the Shoegate Port.[66] This witch, by name 'Alistoun Brathwaite,' used her evil powers on the fair Ermentrude, and enraged her jealousy to fury and a desire for revenge, and presented her with a potion, and a cunning, well-wrought dagger.

"The witch threw a spell over Ermentrude, and took all the good within her away, and implanted evil passions within her breast. It seems that Marie of Mailross slept in this old room, and one night Ermentrude, willed by the witch, went to Marie's bedside, and planted the dagger in her heart, and she died. It seems Ermentrude disappeared, and was never

---

[66] The West Port. The Shoegate or Shoegait was also an old name for South Street.

seen or heard of again, and was supposed to have drowned herself at the Maiden Rock — hence the name it bears.

"That," said Saedeger, "is my quaint tale. The room I slept in was the very room in which in ages past, Marie was done to death by Ermentrude, and it seems to have been my lot to see Ermentrude and discover the secret that lay in that old cupboard."

We all thanked Saedeger, and after thoughtfully consuming a few more whiskies and sodas, and a few more cigars, went off to the Links pondering deeply.[67]

---

[67] There is the ghost of a Blue Lady in Queen Mary's House and the ghost of a Blue Girl in a house in North Street. The latter is often seen by holidaymakers.

A Very Peculiar House

Last time I visited Cambridge I was invited by a friend to meet a party of merry undergraduates. They had all nicknames, and what their real names were I cannot remember. There was Mike, and Whiffle, Toddie, Bulger, the Infant, Eddie Smith from Ramsgate, and the Coal Scuttle. We had a most sumptuous repast, as only can be supplied by first-class Cambridge kitchens, and to which we did ample justice. We were smoking after lunch when they informed me that they had taken the liberty of making an engagement for me to go to tea with such a dear old lady called Sister Elfreda at a house in Bridge Street, opposite St Clement's Church, on the following day at 4.30, as she wished to tell me some ghostly experiences she had had at St Andrews. Of course I said I would very gladly go. They asked me before I went if I could take them behind the scenes that night at the Cambridge Theatre. This I had to flatly refuse, as no undergraduates are allowed within the sacred precincts of the stage door. Next day was a damp, raw, typical Cambridge day. I wended my way to Bridge Street, and easily found the house I was going to, as I had once lodged there. The rooms were kept by two old women who might be called decayed gentlewomen. Their name was Monkswood, and they had been nicknamed "The Cruets," namely, "Pepper" and "Vinegar." Very different from them was their niece, a lovely young actress, who was known on the stage as Patricia Glencluse, who was quite the rage in musical comedy, and who, it was rumoured abroad, would soon become a Duchess. The door was opened by Patricia herself, who said, "Oh, I thought it might be you. Sister Elfreda told me you were coming to tea. You will like her she is such a darling – just like the "Belle of New York," only grown older. If you write anything about what she tells you, mind you send it to me, to the Whittington Company, Theatre, Birmingham." "Of course I will," I said, "and I will put you in it." "Now come along upstairs and I will introduce you to her," she said. She tapped at a door and then opened it, and ushered me into the presence of the Sister. "Look here. Sister," said Patricia, "I have brought the ghost man from St. Andrews to see you. Here he is." "Very good of you," said the Sister as she shook hands with me warmly. "You know," she said, "I have read all your ghost tales." She then told Patricia to run downstairs and send the servant up with tea. Then we seated ourselves down to tea and muffins, and the old lady related her story. She said: - "I wanted very much to tell you of a little experience I had some months ago. I was asked to come up for a short time to look after an invalid lady who lived at St. Andrews. Well, I arrived safely there, and went from the station to the house in a bus. It was an old house, and when I entered I felt a queer sort of creepy sensation come over me such as I had never experienced before. I was ushered into the presence of my host and hostess and the invalid lady. He was a splendid example of an old British soldier, and his wife was a pretty, fragile-looking old piece of china. The invalid lady I found only suffered from nerves, and very little wonder, I thought, in such a peculiar house. I had always a fancy that some other human being resided in the house; but if so, it only remained a feeling. The name of the cook was Timbletoss, the butler was Corncockle, and oddly enough they both came from Cambridge." "What curious names there are here," I said to the Sister; "when I first went to Cambridge I thought the names over the shops must be some gigantic joke – a man once suggested to me that someone must have been specially engaged to come to Cambridge and invent those wonderful names." "Well," continued the Sister, "it really was a most extraordinary house. I had never seen anything out of the common before, and I have never seen anything like that house since. The servants told me most remarkable tales – how the bedclothes were twitched off the bed in the night by unseen hands, and how the tables and chairs rattled about over the floor, and the knives and forks flew off the table. Curious little coloured flames known there as 'Burbilangs' used to float about in the air at night, and Corncockle, the butler, said the beer taps in the cellar were constantly turned on and the gas turned off. The servants had to have their wages considerably raised to keep them in the house. At luncheon on several occasions the lady used to jump up and run out of the room in great haste, and did not reappear till dinner, when she looked very white and shaky. On two occasions I was ordered to go at once to my room and lock the door and remain there until the old Squire sounded the hall gong. They seemed very much perturbed when I got down again. I will only mention one or two curious things I saw. One was a quaint creature called the 'Mutilated Football,' which stotted downstairs in front of me, and when it reached the lobby a head and a pair of arms and legs appeared, and it pattered off down the cellar stairs at a breakneck speed. The story goes that this creature was once a great athlete and football player, and when he got old and fat would insist on still playing, though warned not to do so. He got such a severe kick that his ribs were broken, and he died on the field. I never heard the true story of the 'Animated Hairpin,' but I saw it once seated in an armchair in the dining-room. It looked as if it had on black tights and a close-fitting black jersey. It had a very long white face, with great round eyes like an owl's and black hair standing on end to a great height. When it saw me it got up quickly from the chair, bowed very low till its head nearly touched the ground, and then walked in a most stately manner out of the room. Then I saw 'The Green Lady' – a tall, beautiful girl with very long hair and a rustling green brocaded dress. She glided along as if on wheels. That this was no imagination of mine may be drawn from the fact that one day when I had a little girl to tea she suddenly clutched my arm and asked me who that beautiful lady in green with the long hair was, who had gone past the door on roller skates. I will not enlarge now on the bangings, crashes, thumpings, and tappings that resounded through the rooms at all times of day and night, sometimes on the ceilings, sometimes on the walls, and sometimes on the floors. The doors and windows, too, had a nasty habit of suddenly opening without any visible cause; and another very curious thing was that one might be sitting by a very bright fire when, without any apparent cause, it would suddenly go out, and leave nothing but inky blackness. The first night I slept in my room in this peculiar house I examined it most thoroughly, but there was nothing out of the common to be seen. My door, which I most carefully locked, flew open with a bang, though the bolt still remained out. I again closed and relocked the door, and put a chair against it, but to my astonishment the door once more flew open and hurled the chair across the room. After that I decided to leave the door wide open and see what would happen next. I got quite accustomed to the 'Burbilangs' or flying lights – they were like pretty fireworks. Nothing more happened to me for several days, till one morning I awoke about two o'clock to find a youngish-looking monk seated in an arm- chair, 'Fear not,' he said, 'Sister Elfreda, I left this earth many years ago. In life my name was Walter Desmond, but when I became a monk at St. Anthony I was known as Brother Stanilaus. As a rule I am invisible, but can assume my bodily shape if necessary. In life I was at St. Andrews, Durham, and Cambridge.' 'When in Cambridge,' I asked, 'did you know the writer of St. Andrews ghost stories?' 'No, I only knew him by sight. I was very young then, and was somewhat afraid of him, as I heard when getting on the Links he used to become very violent if he missed a putt, topped a drive, foozled an iron shot, or got into any of the numerous ditches which intersect the Cambridge Links. But I came specially to see you tonight to tell you how to rid this house of the evil influence there is over it. I have here a manuscript regarding it which I took from a foreign library, and which I wish you to read and act upon, and so purify this house and

130

render it habitable, but I must impose the strictest secrecy on you in regard to what you read; reveal it to no one.' 'But how will you get that paper back?' I asked the brother. 'Oh, time and space are nothing to us – I got this paper from that distant library only a few seconds ago, and when you have digested it, it will be immediately replaced from whence it came; only follow all the directions carefully, or my visit will have been of no avail. We read the paper over together most carefully, but of that I may say no more.' 'Having told you what to do,' said the monk, 'I fear I must hie[68] hence. I have much to do tonight after replacing the paper.' 'I will fulfil all that you have asked me brother,' I said, 'and hope that it will make this house less fearsome. But before you go, brother,' I said, 'as you are a Cambridge man, why do you not pay a visit to the author of St. Andrews Ghost Stories?' 'He would not see me because I would not materialise myself there, I could only appear as a puff of smoke, or, as it were, a light fog.' ('Thanks, Sister,' I said, 'do not ask any nasty damp fogs to come and call on me.' She laughed.) The monk, in vanishing, said, 'Remember, Sister, no bolts, locks, or bars can keep us from going where we choose.'"

I got up and thanked her, and proceeded to put on a greatcoat. "I never wear greatcoats," I said, "in Scotland, but I am afraid of the Cambridge damp, so I borrowed this topcoat from Colonel Churchtimber."

"You have dropped something out of the pocket," said the Sister.

"Hullo," I said, "this is a piece of classical music which must belong to Macbeth Churchtimber, the Colonel's son. Now, goodnight, and many thanks. Sister Elfreda."

I descended the stairs and said goodnight to the Cruets and Patricia. As I wandered down the street to the theatre in the damp foggy evening I pondered over what Sister Elfreda had told me, and as I lit my pipe I kept thinking of those people – "The Mutilated Football," "The Animated

---

[68] hasten

Hairpin," and the "Monk Brother Stanilaus," to whom locks, bolts and bars were as nothing, and who had the nasty habit of appearing to his friends as a damp cloud – a habit, I think, not to be encouraged.

* * * * * *

Sister Elfreda now informs me that the peculiar house is now quite "normal," and that all the "bogies" have vanished into thin air.

THE STRANGE STORY

OF

ST ANDREWS HAUNTED TOWER

BY

Dean of Guild
W. T. LINSKILL

1925

Introduced
by
Richard Falconer

William Linskill (left), Mr Ferguson (middle)
Captain Daniel Wilson (right)[69]

This rare photograph was taken in 1921 in the bar of the Star
Hotel. It was called the New Bar until this year when its name
changed to the Star Bar that would eventually become the
Star. The photo features three keen golfing friends and
drinking buddies, William Linskill, Mr Ferguson, the owner
of the hotel at that time, and one Captain Daniel Wilson.

Based in St Andrews, Captain Daniel Wilson, otherwise
known as 'Captain Dan', was the Captain of Clipper Ships.
In 1892, he sailed from Scotland to Australia and back on
the maiden voyage of the ship Stoneleigh. It took him two

---

[69] Image reproduced courtesy of the St Andrews Preservation Trust

years. For its second voyage he was transferred to another boat, a fortunate occurrence; Stoneleigh sank in the Tasman Sea in 1895 with all hands lost. With a number of near misses, he was the last of the old sea fairing captains in St Andrews. Remember Linskill also had a near miss with the Tay Bridge Disaster.

Captain Dan died in 1926, aged 82, but not at sea. He was in a collision involving a lorry whilst riding pillion on a motorcycle in Fife. It was Captain Dan who gave Linskill one of the earlier recorded reports we have of the physical body of the White Lady being seen in a chamber of Hepburn's Wall. I have placed the time-period as being around 1849 after the turret light-house resumed operation, but his reference to what the boys saw could well apply to many years before this period, as well as to many occasions after, but not beyond 1861. The full account will be found on p.141.

Linskill was greatly fascinated by the Haunted Tower and the White Lady. He was one of the keenest correspondents to the newspapers about her, and the two short *fictional* stories he published about her in *St Andrews Ghost Stories* served to further promote what was already a very famous ghost, not just locally, but internationally. The White Lady gripped the imagination of St Andrews, Scotland, Britain and abroad.

On October 5th, 1925, he wrote a lengthy article for the *St Andrews Citizen* titled: *St Andrews Wonderful Old Haunted Tower*. Following his death in 1929, this became a 31-page booklet in 1938, reproduced here for the first time and titled: *The Strange Story of St Andrews Haunted Tower*. The *Citizen* reprinted a short part of it as a promotional advertisement for the booklet in the same year.

The article primarily comprises newspaper excerpt's spanning back to 1893, covering interviews and correspondence between those who present at the 1868 opening of the Haunted Tower that then generated a great deal of correspondence and speculation right up to 1925 from those having read about the openings in the press, then sharing their thoughts and theories as to what had been discovered.

There are also letters and excerpts from c.1849 to 1861 of those who had seen the White Lady corpse in passing or through repairs to the precinct wall. Linskill picks up the accounts from c.1849 to 1888.

I have included his article here as it gives a flavour and introduction to a little-known unfolding mystery. It is only when the detail is looked at in depth that a great many complexities and misunderstandings arise for who saw what, when, and most importantly where.

The first account of the White Lady corpse being seen was in 1826. Linskill doesn't give mention to it in his article, but it is very important and more accurate than some of the later descriptions press editors found easy to embellish, so I have recorded it here:

'A few explorers, who, on desiring to see what lay beyond the sealed chamber of the Haunted Tower, apprehensively gathered in secret early one morning to open it. A Professor of the United College in North Street headed the exploration. When they went in, they were amazed at what they found. It appears the chamber was the hiding place of up to 10 coffins dating from different centuries. There were nine males and one female. Some were wrapped head to toe in white wax cloth, including that of a slim corpse, four and a half feet long. Under the wax cloth wrappings was the corpse of a woman, young and beautiful. She wore a long white silk dress, and it was as if she had fallen asleep that very hour. [She was also wearing long white leather calf-skin gloves and had long black hair.] Both she and the other corpses were in a perfect state of preservation. There was no obvious indication as to their identities, or why they should be entombed within the tower. Following a cursory examination, the Professor went to the Lord Advocate and told him of their discovery. He immediately ordered them to leave the bodies alone in their tomb and reseal the chamber'.

Archaeology as we know it, didn't appear until Carter in 1921 and his discoveries in Egypt. Before then it was thought of as desecration to tamper with the dead. Consequently, many elements from within the Haunted Tower that could give us valuable historical clues were ignored or destroyed. The remnants of the corpses and coffins for example were disposed of into a hole in the ground at some point during the First World War, with no suggestion as to its locality. All one can assume is they would have been buried (unceremoniously) in the Cathedral precincts. There is no record. The middle chamber was then used as a tool shed for the workmen.

My book *A St Andrews Mystery*, 2015, is 266 pages devoted to unravelling what you are about to read. It concerns various openings of the Haunted Tower, what they found and when. All the newspaper excerpts Linskill incorporates in this article will be found in full in that volume, alongside a great deal more that serves to fill in a great many historical gaps.

There was a minefield of information I had to untangle. Not least the 1893 interviews, with many crossed wires that no one has ever picked up. It led me to realise there are two physical corpses of a White Lady, and they share very similar descriptions, but with subtle differences. One was wearing more expensive items. She has been more well-hidden within an inner sanctum, and was given more care for her internment and preservation. I believe she is still present.

My conclusions are based on my researches and subsequent research since 2015. It will be found in my *History of St Andrews* to be published 2022, including where she is hidden and who she may be, which you may read about in the press if archaeological permissions are granted to locate her – although it will be a lengthy process.

If the following generates your interest, for all the information *A St Andrews Mystery* contains, I do recommend you reading it. When I published it in 2015, the *Citizen* described it as "Richard's latest fictional book." They never read my brief, and I guess they were not expecting a nonfiction work to come out about the White Lady. Of course it was fiction, how could it not be? Unfortunately, their mistake was a grave error that would prove contrary to the motivation of most who would then buy it. In one respect it is a pity it wasn't fiction, I could have saved myself over 30 years of research up to its publication.

When these reports were being presented, the mistake everyone made, including Linskill, was to assume the descriptions of the While Lady corpse were simply conflicting. In fact, they didn't even get that far. They're not. For you to gain an idea about this second corpse, view the conflicting descriptions as being from two different corpses, in two different chambers, and ignore any suggestion of their all being from the middle chamber of the Haunted Tower. That was just the assumption they all made. You will then see there are two completely separate accounts, and each with their own correlations. It will all then start falling into place as you begin to understand what the Victorian antiquarians unfortunately missed.

THE STRANGE STORY

OF

ST ANDREWS HAUNTED TOWER

BY

Dean of Guild
W. T. LINSKILL

1925

Printed in booklet form 1938
Republished here for the first time

Nonfiction

ANYTHING quite out of the beaten track or common every day rut makes a strong appeal to the minds of ordinary mortals. They love new sensations. Something very, very, very ancient like the wonderful Egyptian tombs creates great curiosity and wonderment. Historical, Antiquarian, and especially supernatural matters can fascinate most minds unless they are totally lacking in imagination. What on this earth can be more interesting than hunting for buried old ruins, concealed treasure, crypts, hypogeum's,[70] dungeons, vaults, oubliettes or tricky winding subterranean passages, stores of deep mystery, and of many queer tricks and pitfalls? What imaginable thing can possibly be more thrilling and exciting than unravelling the mystic tangled web of the awesome wonders of haunted castles or haunted rooms and avenues, and investigating the real cause, nature, appearance, and manners of the supposed ghostly appearances? Trying to get at the real truth of these matters needs nerve, strong will, persistence, pluck, and dour determination. Such investigations are continually going on, privately, day by day all over the world, although we may hear little about them. Sometimes they are ultimately crowned with success. All honour to such intrepid explorers – whatever line of investigation they may take up. The humblest efforts sometimes reveal the unexpected in most mysterious ways, far beyond the comprehension of most folk. Miracles have never really ceased, but continue daily in our midst, often unknown, unheeded, and unsolved. We have still very much to learn.

One of the Mysteries of St Andrews.

"One of the many mysteries of St Andrews is without doubt "The Haunted Tower" – that square tower beyond the

---

[70] Underground chambers

Lighthouse Turret in Hepburn's great Abbey Wall. There is a deep mystery and romance about this solid, squat, square tower and its former contents: it somehow reminds one of the Capulet Vault or tomb in "Romeo and Juliet" (But the middle chamber in the Haunted Tower was never intended as a tomb), and makes one wonder who was the satin-clad Juliet who lay sleeping in this chamber, and whether there was any Romeo connected with her and her early death. That she was someone of importance – and of great importance – is certain. But what a strange resting-place she had among many others of clearly different periods!

By the way, the old gateway at the Light-house round tower [situated just east of the haunted tower] had, it is stated [no reference], a statue of the Holy Mother over its arch, and that the emblematic pot of lilies on the Haunted Tower make me fancy that both gateway and tower may have been dedicated to her, as is also the Church of St Mary on the Kirkhill close by. [The small and exclusive sacred Chapel between the high altar and the eastern gable was also dedicated to her and was known as the Lady Chapel.]

Peeping into the Chamber of Corpses.

Captain Daniel Wilson, a well-known St Andrean, informs me that many years ago his father was custodian of the turret light-house. He had several brothers and each of them had in turn to light and extinguish this lamp. [71] In those

---

[71] The Catholics created a powerful light here by supplying it with wood and coal as a beacon for shipping. With the Reformation, the light went out and the lighthouse wasn't used again until 290 years later in 1849. This is when Captain Wilson's father and brothers maintained it, and unlike their Catholic predecessors, they powered it by gas lighting. The lighthouse, a fixed beacon, was in operation right up until the mid 1940s when the Coastguard watchtower/lighthouse was created by the former eastern gable of St Mary on the Rock overlooking the harbour.

days of long ago, Hepburn's Abbey Wall was thickly covered with the most luxurious ivy [it was still present in the 1920s, but may have been more extensive along the length of the perimeter wall] and it was a great bird-nesting rendezvous for the laddies of the past. There were several gaps and chinks then in the solid masonry of the mystic old Haunted Tower, and the boys enjoyed peering through these gaps and seeing with awe and wonder the form of a lovely girl robed all in white lying stretched out in her coffin within that tower. The lid, an early cope-shaped affair, had apparently slipped off, and lay on the chamber floor beside the coffin, exposing to view the form of the young girl who had very beautiful features to the awe-stricken gazers, who, after peering in, used to flee in terror.

A Place Dreaded in the Dark.

In those days few people cared to pass that tower of mystery alone after nightfall, for it was known that there lay enshrined in it this lovely white maiden, and the attendant well-preserved skeletons or mummies which must have gone through some embalming process. People used to run for their lives when passing this tower at night; and the older fisher folk have told me some hair-raising uncanny stories of awesome sounds and sights that had been heard and seen by many at that Tower. My tutor, Mr Robb, told me some really awful tales about this place.

An Accidental Discovery.

The Rev. Mr Skinner, who many years ago was first Priest of St Andrew's Episcopal church, in Queen's gardens, stated in a letter to the late Mr T. T. Oliphant of Queen Mary's [1860] (and which the latter permitted me to read and copy) that one day when passing the so-called haunted Tower he was watching some workmen repairing the old wall, when one of the masons let his chisel slip inside. On taking out some stones, Mr Skinner stated, a vault or chamber was seen within, and lying in a coffin, with a roof shaped lid beside it, was the figure of a young female handsomely dressed in satin, and having on her arms long gauntlet gloves. The hole was immediately built up again. I have seen, years ago, a portion of one of the gloves which one explorer took away as a trophy of his visit.

Stories of a White Robed Lady.

I might mention here that when I first came to St Andrews nearly 53 years ago, I heard innumerable stories of a white robed girl who haunted the Cathedral and its precincts, but in no way did I connect her then with the Tower Lady. A lady who then lived in Abbey Walk told me she constantly saw a female in trailing white garments walking on the top of the old Abbey Wall, and some of my informant's friends had also witnessed the same occurrence. Three fishermen told me that when coming up one moonlight night from their boats they saw through the iron gate near the Lighthouse the figure of female in white wandering down the path. They thought she must have got locked into the grounds. Imagine their amazement when she glided through the bars of the locked gate. One of the fishermen swooned away: the others threw down their creels and bolted. I heard many more of these yarns.

This old Haunted Tower and its white girl had been almost forgotten when the embers of the of the old romance were once more fanned into flame by a remarkable article that appeared in a number of "The Saturday Review," headed:

"The True Story of the Cathedral Turret."

The writer tells how several gentlemen. Wishing to clear up the mystery of the Haunted Tower, several gentlemen forced a hole in the wall:

"One of the party squeezed in his head and shoulders and all of him, in fine, but his feet. Suddenly they became rigid; and his friends, pulling him out, found that he had fainted. While he was being attended to, a second man peered into the black hole in a like manner, and he too was pulled out in a very ill condition. Finally, a Professor of the United College forced his entire person into the cavity, and did not faint; but presently re-appeared, with the corpse of a woman in his arms, from which the life seemed to have gone but that hour. The turret was now fully explored; and sitting round in a circle, were found twelve bodies, decked as at a feast, and all of them untouched of decay [that description is fiction]."

This article called forth s tremendous lot of letters in various papers, and many prominent citizens in St Andrews were interviewed.

A Dundee reporter called on Mr Jesse Hall, the then gas manager, who is the local representative of the Woods and Forests Department. Mr Hall said he had heard about the article in "The Saturday Review," and remarked: - "I have been about the ruins since 1845, more or less, and I will tell you all I know about this Tower. It is situated on the wall next to the Scores, a short distance from the tower with the light on it. There has been a parapet wall along the whole of the Cathedral Wall, but it is nearly all down now, and the pathway goes right through the turret in question. This turret seems to have been roofed, though none of the roofing remains. It is, however, the best preserved of the lot. About the time that the first entrance into the tower was effected [1868] we had been engaged in levelling down the grounds, and had lowered the surface for a couple of feet."

When the Chamber was opened.

Here is an extract from a book of jottings belonging to the late Mr Smith, watchmaker [1801- 1873][72]: - "Square Tower on north wall of the Cathedral grounds - This tower had often been an object of curiosity to me, and I felt anxious to examine the interior. Old people call it the Haunted Tower. The tower projects a considerable space from the line of the wall on both sides, and has had a stair leading up to a doorway, which is built up. I had frequently asked Mr Hall, the Inspector, to make an opening to see the interior, and on 7th September, 1868[73] he, along with Walker, myself, and T. Carmichael, mason (it was Grieve) made an opening in the doorway sufficient to get in. We found it a square chamber, with a recess westward in the body of the wall, in which was a number of coffins containing bodies, the coffins being piled one over the other. The bodies – about 10 in number – which we examined, were in a wonderful state of preservation. They had become dried and sufficiently stiff to be lifted up and set on end. Some of them appeared to have been wrapped in linen, and must have undergone a sort of embalming. One of them, a female, had on her hands white leather gloves, very entire, a piece of which Carmichael took away as a relic. some of these coffins were of oak, some had been ridge-topped (this shows their age), and in some were remains of waxcloth. Nothing was found to indicate who they were or when they had been laid there."

---

[72] Mr David Couper Smith, was a watch and clock maker with a shop and workshop at 95 South Street, St Andrews. Known as "Tickie Smith" he died five years after the 1868 opening in 1873, so his report wasn't written long after the opening. His business was succeeded by his son, also called David.

[73] This was 42 years after the start of the initial clearing of rubble in the Cathedral precincts and the start of the speculation as to its purpose.

Mr Hall continued his story thus:- "Well, I am not sure about Carmichael, I think it must have been John Ainslie. He had been pointing the walls, and the stone gave way. He looked in and

Got a Scare,

and then told me about the hole. The hole was built up at that time without the vault being opened. Unfortunately, I did not keep a note of the dates, so that I do not know when that would be; but Mr Smith, watchmaker, and Mr Walker, the University Librarian [The University Library was the King James Library in South Street, opposite Mr Smiths clock shop], who were both antiquaries, but are now dead, pressed me frequently to allow them to open the vault. I did not care about it, as I did not like to disturb the dead; but I at last consented, and early one summer morning before six o'clock – as we did not want to make it public – the three of us, Mr Smith, Mr Walker and myself, went to the place and made a small hole, just enough to admit a man's head and shoulders. The doorway opened into a passage, and round the corner to the left was the vault proper. We all scrambled in, and by the light of a candle, which we carried, we saw two chests lying side by side. [And others piled on top of each other.] I cannot say how many chests there were. We did not want to disturb them any more than we could help. There would be half-a-dozen as far as I can remember. I saw the body of a girl. The body was stiff and mummified like. What appeared to be a glove was on one of the hands."

Mr Hall was asked what became of the body of the girl? He replied – "I don't know. After we went in the first time we shut up the hole and kept the matter a profound secret, and I did not know that anyone knew of it except ourselves. People had been in the habit of calling the place the Haunted Tower, and when going to the harbour they ran past it. No one had any idea that it was a place of burial till we opened it."

Curious Skulls.

The late Professor Heddle, was interviewed on the subject. He said that he and Dr Traill[74] saw a large number of skulls which had been found in the lower part of the Haunted Tower: - "We found that not one of these individuals could ever have had toothache. Their teeth were in splendid condition. Then we found that in some of them the Atlas bone – that is the last bone of the vertical column was anchylosed to the skull (that is, there was a bone union instead of a cartilaginous one), so that none of these poor fellows could have turned their heads without turning their bodies. Another curious thing was that in the case of about a dozen skulls the lower jaw was tied up with silk banana handkerchiefs, in which there were bleaching holes." The Professor[75] also stated that he put his head and body into the upper chamber. He saw the piled-up coffins and the nearest one body, the head of which was lying back as if it had broken off the body. He put his hand on a deep-chested man. The body was wholly converted into adipocere – that is, a fatty substance.[76]

There were most wonderful stories written about the Tower. One was headed –

---

[74] Dr William Traill, St Andrews University. Like Heddle, he was a member of the St Andrews Literary and Philosophical Society.

[75] Professor Matthew Forster Heddle (1828-1897). Professor of Chemistry in St Andrews from 1862 and a noted mineralogist in his day. Based in the United College at St Salvator's, he collected quite a number of the famous Dura Den fossil fish. Prominent member of the St Andrews Literary and Philosophical Society and one of Linskill's antiquarians.

[76] Adipocere is a greyish white or brown waxy substance formed during the decomposition of a corpse lying in a moist place of burial. Also known as corpse, grave or mortuary wax, it is created by a reaction occurring between moisture and the body's fatty acids and calcium soaps.

"A Girl Mummy in the Chamber of Horrors!"

I came on the scene on the top of it all, and wrote my midnight experiences to the papers at full length. I must quote a few remarks I wrote from Cambridge at that time.

"Since I can first remember St Andrews as a wee laddie there have always been the most absurd and fantastic fairy tales told about the so-called Haunted Tower. I could cover sheets of foolscap with the absolute nonsense I have heard from time to time. One man, a pious and worthy person told me that within that Tower reposed the incorruptible body of a sweet girl saint."

Another writer speculated thus: -
"Who shall say what sacred relics may have been enclosed in this secret vault (*Linskill's note: it was not secret – just the opposite*) so rudely broken in upon and so sacrilegiously handled – perhaps those of the Patron Saint of Scotland, perhaps of the Pictish Princess, Muren, the first according to the legend of St Andrew to be buried at Kilrymont? [77] Princess Muren, the daughter of King Constantine, who resigned his crown to become Abbot of the Culdee Church on the Kirkhill, was very probably embalmed and kept in that early church; but why on earth after all those years should she be the mysterious girl enshrined in the Haunted Tower?"

---

[77] Kilrymonth or Kilrymont was an early name for St Andrews. There are a few variations for its meaning including 'Church on the King's Hill or Mount', or 'End of the Kings Hill' as this was a Royal Centre for the Pictish Kings, but there are also older druidic associations than the Picts.

The Tower Opened at Midnight.

On the 21st of August, 1888, at midnight, I opened up the tower. Among others I had with me was Grieve, who when a lad and an apprentice mason opened the Tower for Mr Hall, Mr Smith, Mr Walker, and others of whom I have spoken. When I got in I found the whole of the interior in most dire confusion. Wood and bits of coffins were flung about all over the place, and rather well preserved skeletons were lying here and there and a lot of loose skulls. When Grieve the mason saw the place, he said – "Oh! that's all quite changed, not a bit like I saw it years ago when I helped to open it." [1868]. He showed me the corner where the bonny lassie had been resting, and told me she lay there with her long hair just as if she was taking her sleep – not a bit like death – and her dress was beautiful. It puzzles one to imagine the actual personality of this youthful and bonny Juliet laid to rest in such a strange place with such strange companions and surroundings. None of the occupants of this chamber in the tower had ever really been buried. Many persons absolutely refuse to be deposited below the soil, and there are many coffins kept above ground in strange buildings and handsome surroundings. I know of many at home and abroad. One man desired to be laid to rest on the roof of his house. He said he wanted to be up, not down.

The Great Age of the Bodies found in the Tower.

Mr A. Hutcheson, a well-known antiquary – now dead – made some interesting remarks in an article headed: The Haunted Tower, St Andrews," written Broughty Ferry on the 8h of February, 1894. I will quote a few of his remarks.

"If the Abbey Wall cannot claim to be older than the beginning of the 16th Century, I think there are good grounds for believing the interments to be far older than the vault in which they were found in 1868. I base this conclusion on several considerations.. . . . These are brought out in the information which has been published. These are, first, that some of the coffins were of oak, and some of them had been ridge-topped; second, the evidence of embalming; and third, the appearance of the 'wax cloth.' In order that the significance of these features may be realised in a question affecting the age of the interments, it may be well to review the evidences afforded by history. Examples of ridge-topped coffins in stone have been ascribed to the fifth century. The earliest forms were probably those curious mound-shaped examples, something like a boat laid keel uppermost, of which class there are late examples at Meigle and Brechin. By-and-bye the mound or boat form gave way to the roof or ridge-topped form, and there is reason for believing that even inside of churches coffin lids to stand above the floor and mounds of earth were common in very early times. The coped coffin lid, however, held its own against all law, and in the 13th century was very common. It was now highly ornamented, and by the 14th century was frequently elevated on a base, and so led up to the magnificent altar tombs of a later age. Coffins of oak are as old as the Bronze age in Britain; but the ridged or coped oaken lid doubtless came in when stone coffins were placed on or near to the surface, so that the lid would be above the ground, that when the bodies of saints were embalmed their relic might be seen. . . . Richly carved, and ornamented with the precious metals and jewels, such a lid formed a fitting covering, easily removed to exhibit to the faithful the precious relics enshrined within.

The evidence of embalming seem indubitable. The bodies in the Tower, it is said, could be lifted up and set on end. They presented more or less the appearance of mummies. The process of embalming in Christian times was usually performed on the bodies of saints that their relics might be exhibited. It was in these times seldom performed on any but the most exalted in rank or piety. Another indication of age is the waxcloth Mr Smith stated was seen in some of the coffins. This was doubtless the "Cere-Cloth," - a cloth prepared with wax and used as a winding sheet. It is of great antiquity. . . . All of these peculiarities of interment are indicative of ancient modes of burial, which, although occasionally represented in rare instances in the 16th Century, render it unlikely that so many instances of these different practices would be brought together in one set of interments. Moreover, we have the evidence as to the condition of the oak coffins, which are said to have been more decayed than the fur ones, thus pointing to a great age.

A consideration of these circumstances seems to render it impossible to attribute the interments to any part of the 16th century. To account for the aggregation of so many bodies exhibiting the age peculiarities referred to above, some other explanation must be forthcoming than the supposition of ordinary interment, and an interment, be it remembered, in the second storey of a tower."

Andrew Lang and Saints.

About the same time as the above was written a letter appeared from the late Mr Andrew Lang in which he said: - "It is, I think, unlikely that St Andrews ever produced many local saints, nor would a whole saint be readily parted with by other churches. Persons of rank are more probably the inmates of the Haunted Tower. The relics of the Apostle would, I presume, be kept in a reliquary of precious metal, which doubtless did not escape the zeal of the Reformers. Still, the relics may conceivably have been hidden among the bodies."

Then comes a letter of mine from the University Golf Club of Cambridge in which I said that I had read Mr Hutcheson's letter regarding the Haunted Tower in the *Citizen* of 24th February, 1894. Continuing, I wrote: - "It may interest some of your readers to know that I saw in the Crypt of a chapel near Bonn in 1876 (attached to a convent of Servites built in 1627) the bodies of a large number of Capuchin monks in lidless coffins. Although 400 years old, they were in a magnificent state of preservation, the nails on the toes and fingers, and the vestments being almost intact. In the Haunted Tower here the toe and finger nails of some of the bodies were also in a perfect state."

Conflicting Suggestions.

On the 14th March, 1894, Mr David Henry, in the course of a long letter, said: - "It appears to me that the most obvious solution is the right one – namely, that some family of consideration in the city or neighbourhood had taken possession of the Tower as a family mausoleum, and adapted it to their purpose. . . . It was a common mode of disposing of the dead. Private mausoleums exist all over the country in churchyards and in woods and valleys. Within my own knowledge, the chief heritor in a remote parish, not more than half a century ago left instructions in his will that when he, the last of his race and name, was laid within the family mausoleum, the door should be built up. Built up it was, and the whole structure is now going to ruin. Many such cases must occur to those interested in such matters."

There was a case of this kind at Ceres.

On 20th march, 1894, Mr A. Hutcheson wrote: - "With all deference, I cannot see that Mr Henry's 'solution' accounts for the following particulars of interment. Firstly - the coped oak coffins, very much decayed. Can Mr Henry point to the use of coped oak coffins in the 17th Century? Then as to the decay and its suggestiveness. Oak is very well-known to be a very lasting wood. Coffins of oak attributable to the Bronze Age have been discovered in England, Germany, and Denmark. The age claimed for the coffins in the Tower is not on a parallel with these; but a fair inference may be drawn from them in favour of the belief that coffins of oak, dating no further back than the beginning of the 17th century, could scarcely have been very much decayed in 1868. Second - the evidence of vestments, embalming, and cere cloth. I take it these features are established beyond question. Can Mr Henry cite any instances in Scotland attributable to the 17th Century? I have not referred to the gloves which covered the hands of one of the embalmed bodies. This, I consider, is a strong point in favour of my contention. Gloves were usually put on that the faithful might kiss the hands of the canonised person."

"St Andrews Vandalism."

Mr Andrew Lang a few months later, had an article in *"Longmans Magazine"* headed 'St Andrews Vandalism," in which he said: - "The Haunted Tower in the precinct wall was harried and plundered by unintelligent thieves, and the contents were scattered. In the College Museum is a beautiful foot of a woman, an exquisite thing, far lovelier than Trilby's.[78] It is reported to have come out of the Haunted Tower, but nobody can really know the truth."

Grieve, the Mason's Story
Writing from 3 Crail's Lane, St Andrews. James Grieve, the mason, who, as I said before, opened up the Tower for

---

[78] Trilby is a novel by George du Maurier. Published in 1899 the book is about the left foot of a young woman in Paris called 'Trilby'. The book sold a million copies in its day

me, said: - "When about fifteen years of age I assisted John Ainslie (a mason) to open the haunted Tower. I then saw the body of a woman with a silk napkin tied round her head. She was lying on the floor of the Chamber, and the coffin was sticking about three feet above, and the bottom had fallen out. She was in a state of perfect preservation, and had long black hair[79]."

A Skipper's Yarn. [and a yarn it is]

On 31st January, 1894, a letter appeared in the Edinburgh Evening Dispatch, headed

"Another Strange Story of St Andrews."

And signed "Interested reader." The letter commenced: - "While on board a yacht on the Clyde two summers ago which had just been bought and brought there from St Andrews, the skipper, who was a native of that City, told me a story which I did not credit at the time, but since seeing your issue of Monday and to-day's *Scotsman* I think there may be some truth in it. He then goes on to say that this skipper told him that he and some medical students had one night exhumed from an old tower a female body which was in a state of complete preservation. The body was that of a young, good-looking girl, with black hair. It was locked up in a cellar. A rival antiquary got wind of the find, and bribed the skipper to steal it, which was duly done. After this the body was lost sight of.

Personally, I cannot say I believe one word of this skipper's mythical tale, but without doubt between 1868

---

[79] Grieve is the only one to mention her having long black hair - 1861.

(when Mr Hall and his friends explored the Haunted Tower) and 1888 (when my friends and I examined the place) some folks had paid a visit or visits to its interior and played havoc therein, smashed up the coffins, and removed any means of identification.

Two very long letters appeared by one who signed himself "Dean of Tyasaoga," of which I quote one paragraph: - "The strong presumption, therefore, is that the bodies in the tower are not those of any of the Scottish Saints and others, who lived while embalming was a difficult and expensive process, but are the bodies of people of a later age whose position in life was well-known to their contemporaries – members of a kingly stock among whom there was money and influence enough to have their bodies after death treated in this way for preservation."

Another writer, talking of Saints, &c., said: - "This would not apply to the bodies of the Princess Muren and the early founders of Christian Settlements in St Andrews, since these persons would have little or no distinction beyond the limits of St Andrews."

I cannot put into print summaries of all the long letters all holding divergent views of the remains in the mystic Haunted Tower.

A Poem in Memory of the Unknown Lady.

In December, 1894, there appeared leaflet by a local gentleman[80] with a splendid etching of the famous Haunted Tower on it, and the following poem: -

---

[80] The poem was anonymous until 31 years later, when Linskill disclosed the name in his 1925 article. It was written by the late Colonel Thomson. (I have 26 years in *A St Andrews Mystery*, which would place it as 1920, but that was concerning a different article where the poem didn't feature.)

Reflections of a visitor on seeing the foot of a girl embalmed. Or otherwise well preserved, exposed to view in a glass case in the College Museum.

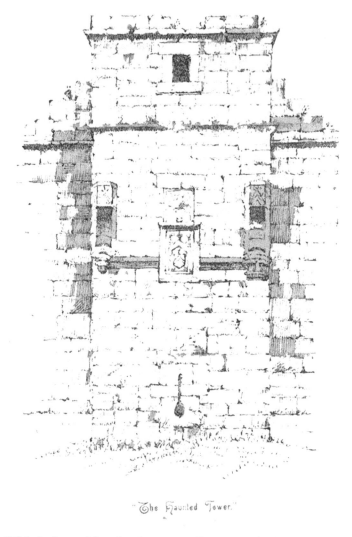

"The Haunted Tower."

[This is the etching for the poem. It was not included in the article or the booklet.]

Whence came this dainty little foot?
A gruesome thing, it doth repel me,
Curator knoweth not, is mute,
And Janitor he cannot tell me.

An object grim, yet it begets
Strange thoughts and eerie speculation,
Queer brooding fancies, vain regrets,
With wonder at its preservation.

For many lustres it has lain
In mouldy grave or mausoleum,
And now it sees the light again
Encased in glass in our Museum.

It once was pink and white as down,
Of sunny peach or ripening cherry;
But now its tint is ruddy brown
As hazel nut or autumn berry.

Some sixteen summers it has seen
Of creeping, toddling, running, dancing;
Has romped and skipped upon the green
The fairy feet like sunbeams glancing.

Oft it has roamed the yellow sands,
And bathed and paddled in the "briny",
While breakers thundered on the strand,
And wavelets kissed the toes so tiny.

In spring, where blooms the primrose sweet,
It sought thy sunny nooks, Kinkell;
When o'er the rocks the little feet
Sprung lightly like a young gazelle.

Its owner's name – Ah! Who can tell?
'Twas surely musical and pretty.
Like Mary, Maud, or Isobel;
Perhaps they called her Lady Betty.

The child of gentle blood, I ween,
Of gallant knight or baron bold;
Her pedigree it might have been
As ancient as the ruins of old.

A bright embodiment of grace,
Displayed in every motion,
Love, candour, beaming in a face
Oft glowing with emotion.

A maiden, winsome, sweet, and sprightly,
With dancing limb and laughing eye –
One who could tread a measure lightly,
And sullen care and grief defy.

Who to the Links would sometimes stray,
With other maids, in summer weather,
To watch the eager golfers play,
'Mid golden gorse and blooming heather.

Or to the ancient butts she'd hie[81]
To see the noble archers shoot,
And 'mong her college friends espy
Some honoured names of high repute:

Bright sons of men of learning,
Bold scions of war and strife,
Blithe lads from the braes of Angus,
Young bonnet Lairds of Fife.

She may have known the gallant Graeme,
Montrose, that flower of chivalrie;
Or later still, of tragic fame,
The brave, the beautiful Dundee.

Her life was one long summer's day,
And she the darling of the hour;
A rosebud in a garden gay –

---

[81] Go quickly

Alas! it never lived to flower.

Poor little foot! there's none can tell
Its owner's sad and simple story –
The cruel fate, the blow that fell
To waft her to the realm of glory.

Note [by Colonel Thomson], - "There is every reason to believe that the foot in question belonged to the mysterious and interesting collection of human remains discovered some thirty years ago [he is speaking of the 1868 opening] entombed and immured in the upper chamber of the quadrilateral tower situated east of the turret light. This tower now vulgarly known as the 'Haunted Tower'[82] which formed part of the wall embracing the Cathedral and other Church property was built by Priors John and Patrick Hepburn early in the 16th Century. How it came to be used for such a purpose as above described and by whom is still shrouded in mystery; but this we know that the objects discovered were of a singularly interesting character. They consisted of coffins of pine and oak of antique shape, containing skeletons; also other coffins of more recent date, enclosing the remains of bodies in various stages of decay – some of them in a state of partial preservation.

Notably of the latter class was one – the corpse of a young female attired in costly grave clothing which appeared to have been embalmed with remarkable success. To this body belonged, I am convinced, the little foot now exposed to view in the College Museum.[83] Since the original discovery by

---

[82] A term popularised by Linskill through his first story about the White Lady. *The Beautiful White Lady of the Haunted Tower.*

[83] The museum had been created by the 'Lit and Phils', an eminent body comprising professors and academics who all jumped ship to join Linskill's Antiquarian Society in his search for the underground passages. Leaving no one to man the museum it closed in 1904 and became the Upper and Lower College Hall. I saw a photo of the foot in the case in an early copy of the *Citizen* and have been unable to find it since.

certain inquisitive citizens of St Andrews, the chamber has been repeatedly entered, and so thoroughly and unscrupulously plundered of its contents that at the present time nothing remains to be seen but a few bones and fragments of coffin boards."

The Mystery remains a Mystery.

The whole affair is most remarkable, and no record or history whatsoever can be found to give the faintest clue as to who these elaborately interred persons may have been or when they were placed in this peculiar chamber – and why? Will we ever get to know who the handsomely dressed young Juliet was... All that we do know is that the shade of this beautiful White Lady is still supposed to hover around her sepulchre in the old Haunted Tower of Hepburn's Abbey Wall, and has been seen by many.

Note. – In very many respects the Haunted Tower is different and superior to the many other turrets in the Abbey Wall. It is largely built of re-used stones from some older buildings. This is particularly noticeable in the canopies or niches for sacred statues. No other tower or turret has stairs and a door in such a position or a small crypt-like room beneath. Where the mural tablet has been inserted has once clearly contained a casement window looking southward on the Priory Cloisters, probably to watch the movements of the monks.[84]

However, I have also seen the foot in the flesh so to speak, and photographed it for *A St Andrews Mystery*, which is where it will be found.
[84] The top two chambers were added after 1516 by Prior John Hepburn as part of the perimeter wall reconstruction. They doubled its height from the wall built in 1300. The stone was from Holy Trinity Church when it stood between the Haunted Tower and St Regulus Church. The church was in operation for 271 years until 1411, when they started building a

new Holy Trinity Church in South Street (consecrated 1412). The original then became a ruin.

Lightning Source UK Ltd.
Milton Keynes UK
UKHW010812031121
393297UK00002B/80